P9-CDX-707

She was as he remembered her ... she was chewing as she moaned to herself and a trickle of blood ran from her mouth down her chin. She stooped to pick up another meat fragment, thrust it between her full lips.

"Susie!" cried Grimes.

She straightened, stared at him. There was no sign of recognition on her face although, he was sure, there was intelligence behind the brown eyes.

"Susie!"

She growled, deep in her throat, sprang for him, clawed hands outstretched. He brought his gun up but it was too late. She knocked it from his grasp. She threw her arms about him in a bearlike hug and her open mouth, with its already bloodstained teeth, went for his throat.

TO
KEEP
THE
SHIP

A. Bertram Chandler

DAW BOOKS, INC.
DONALD A. WOLLHEIM, PUBLISHER

1301 Avenue of the Americas
New York, N. Y.   10019

For Susan—who bears
little resemblance to Susie.

FIRST PRINTING, JUNE 1978

1 2 3 4 5 6 7 8 9

PRINTED IN U.S.A.

Chapter 1

There is a tide in the affairs of men that, taken at the flood, leads on to fortune. But tides have a habit of ebbing—and Grimes's personal tide had ebbed. He wasn't quite on the rocks but he was most definitely stranded and would remain so until he could raise the wherewithal to pay his steadily mounting port dues and various fines and legal expenses. Meanwhile his beloved *Little Sister* was under arrest, with a writ firmly glued to her outer airlock door, and her owner-master had been obliged to seek paid employment. He was long used to three square meals a day with sips and nibbles in between and there is usually a charge for such sustenance. He could have solved all his financial problems by selling the ship—only a deep-space-going pinnace but valuable nonetheless; even as scrap she would have fetched a not so small fortune—but he was stubborn. He could have shipped out as Third Mate of the Interstellar Transport Commission's *Epsilon Draconis*—one of her officers had been involved in a serious ground-car accident when returning to the spaceport after a rather wild party—but did not elect to do so. Firstly, he had been too long in Command to relish the idea of signing on as a junior officer. Secondly, as long as he was the owner of *Little Sister* he wanted to stay where he could keep an eye on her. A spaceship entirely constructed of an isotope of gold is too precious an artifact to be left in the full charge of strangers.

The trouble had started when Far Traveler Couriers (the plural was unjustified but it sounded better), wholly owned and operated by one John Grimes, fairly recent-

5

ly a full Commander in the Interstellar Federation's Survey Service, more recently Master of the Baroness d'Estang's spaceyacht *The Far Traveler,* had contracted to carry a pair of *lerrigans* from Pangst, their native world, to the interplanetary zoo in New Syrtis, capital city of Bronsonia, all charges to be paid on safe delivery of the beasts. Grimes liked most animals and although he was not especially fond of small, quarrelsome dogs was prepared to be friendly with the larger canines.

The *lerrigans* were handsome enough brutes, not unlike a Terran Pekingese dog in appearance, but with zebra-patterned fur and of considerably greater dimensions, being about the size of full grown Alsatians. Grimes, inspecting them before shipment, had been favorably impressed, especially when the animals grinned happily at him. (Human beings are all too liable to misread the facial expressions of members of other species.) He did not anticipate any trouble during the voyage. A supply of canned food was shipped with the animals and, according to the literature that he had been given, they were omnivorous and would appreciate the variation of their diet by occasional scraps from the captain's table. The instructions were very definite on one point. On no account were the beasts to be let out of their cages.

During this short stay on Pangst, Grimes could not spare the time to visit the library to read up on the habits of his living freight. The consignor had not told him much, saying, "Just keep to the book, Captain, and you'll not go wrong." And when it came to books, Grimes thought, he had access to the entire *Encyclopedia Galactica* through *Little Sister's* memory bank; there would be time enough to learn what he needed to know once he was off planet and on trajectory for Bronsonia. As a matter of fact there was a *lerrigan* entry—a very brief one sandwiched between a long article on "Lerner, Peter Frederick," who for most of his long life, had been an obscure politician on New Maine and another long article on "Lervinsky, Ivan Vladimir," at one time Secretary of the Reformed Communist Party of New

Georgia. *Lerrigans,* Grimes discovered (as though he
didn't know already) were pseudo-canines native to
Pangst.

Pseudo or not, he thought, they were just dogs—big
dogs and friendly. They watched him as he went about
his business in the cabin of the pinnace. They whined—a
most melodious whine—ingratiatingly. They were effu-
sively grateful when he pushed their dishes of food, at the
prescribed intervals, through the spring traps in the heavy
metal mesh of their cages. They cooperated intelligently when he pulled out the trays at the base of their
prisons to dispose of the soiled bedding and to replace
it with fresh. They answered to the names that he had
given them—Boy for the male and Girl for the female.

To hell with the instructions, he thought. They should
be given the opportunity to get some exercise. What
harm could it do? They couldn't possibly run away.
Little Sister herself was cage enough.

So he let the *lerrigans* out of their boxes. They were
ecstatically grateful, whining so musically that Grimes
thought that there should have been words to their
song. They put their front paws on his shoulders and
licked his face. Grimes would have resented such attentions from the pair of *real* dogs but the breath of these
animals was oddly fragrant—intoxicating, almost. They
accompanied him as he went about such duties as he
was obliged to carry out in this almost fully automated
ship, watching him as he checked the position in the
chart tank, as he made his routine inspection of the
mini-Mannschenn and the inertial drive, as he punched
the menu for his evening meal on the keyboard of the
autochef. He had learned by watching their reactions
to the leftovers of previous meals what human foods
they liked so included a double serving of steak, rare.
(*Little Sister's* tissue-culture vats were well stocked.)

Dinner over, he lit his foul pipe and sat in an easy
chair to watch and listen to a program of Carinthian
light opera on his playmaster. This art form—if art
form it could be called—was too corny for cultured
tastes, but Grimes, when he was in what he called his

simple spaceman mood, liked it. He was oddly content as he sprawled there, flanked by the two faithful (as he was already thinking of them) animals. He was more content than he ever had been on the occasions when he had carried human passengers.

Finally he decided to turn in. He considered briefly returning the *lerrigans* to their cages, then decided against it. He did, however, make sure that the doors to the engine space and to the tiny control room were shut. The animals could not possibly do any harm in the main cabin. They could return to sleep in their boxes if they so desired but he would be quite happy if they stretched out on the deck beside his bunk. He stripped, dimmed the cabin lights and then stretched out on the resilient mattress. He was asleep almost at once.

He dreamed, vividly.

He had not thought about Maggie Lazenby for some quite considerable time but he was dreaming about her now. In the dream she was naked, just as he was in reality, and her body was pressed to his and she was kissing him. Her breath was intoxicatingly fragrant. He felt himself stiffening, knew in some remote corner of his mind that this was only a dream and that he would very soon be achieving a lonely climax. But it was a long time since he had had a woman and the dream was a good one. What if his bedsheet were semen-stained? The ship's laundry facilities were better than merely adequate.

It was the knowledge that the lovemaking was only imaginary that saved him. He thrust upward into the dream Maggie's receptive body—and he felt teeth. He screamed, desperately rolled away from under the furry succubi. Scrabbling claws scored his back and the fangs that, had he not fully awoken in time, would have castrated him bit deeply into his right buttock. "Lights!" he yelled, and responsive to his command, the illumination of the cabin came on at full strength. The abrupt transition from near darkness to harsh effulgence dazed the *lerrigans*—not for long but for long enough. Grimes reached for the secret locker that, during a visit to Electra, he had caused to be installed under his bunk. The panel that was its door was sensitive only to the pattern of his fingerprints. It flew open and he grabbed what was in the little cupboard, a Minetti automatic pistol. He had thought that he might, one day, require this weapon for protection against some homicidally inclined human passenger—couriers very often have odd customers—but never dreamed that it would be used against animals.

He thought all this later, when he was cleaning up the mess after treating his wounds. At this moment his main concern was the preservation of his life. He was in an awkward position, crouched by the side of his bunk, pistol in hand, his back to the snarling beasts. He brought his right hand around so that the weapon was pointing behind him, pressed the firing stud. The Minetti jumped in his grasp as the full clip of fifty rounds was discharged, spraying the area to his rear with the tiny but deadly flechettes.

Then he turned. The *lerrigans* were dead, very dead, their green blood soaking into the rich, purple carpet. The male, Grimes noticed with disgust, still had an enormous erection and the female, her haunches upraised, was obviously receptive.

He threw up, adding to the mess on the carpet, then went to the medical cabinet to spray his bites and scratches with antiseptic coagulant.

Little Sister possessed the capability to carry frozen cargo. Grimes, after he was partially recovered, dragged the bodies of the two animals into a refrigerated chamber. They would not now be of any great use to the New Syrtis Zoo but a skilled taxidermist might be able to pretty up the corpses well enough to render them suitable for exhibition in a museum. As for himself, he did not now expect the red carpet to be rolled out for him on his arrival at New Syrtis.

But he did not anticipate the very serious trouble that he had gotten himself into.

Chapter 2

The Director of the New Syrtis Zoo was not pleased. (Grimes had not really expected that he would be.) He took prompt steps to ensure that the freight on the *lerrigans* was not paid and then, after an exchange of Carlottigrams with the consignors on Pangst, brought suit against Grimes for breach of contract, gross negligence and the wanton destruction of protected fauna.

Grimes went to see the Planetary Secretary of the Astronauts' Guild, of which body he was a dues-paying member. Captain Wendover, the secretary, was sympathetic.

He said, "You realize, of course, Captain, that we cannot represent you in your capacity as a shipowner, although we are bound to do so in your capacity as a shipmaster. From what you have told me it was as a shipmaster you acted, and as a shipmaster you got into trouble." He paused, looking at Grimes over his wide desk, an elderly, soberly clad gentleman who had more the appearance of a minister of one of the more puritanical religions than a spaceman. "Now, you say that you were given literature regarding the care and feed of the animals before your departure from Pangst. In this was there any mention of . . . er . . . sexual peculiarities?"

"No, Captain. Here. You can read for yourself."

"Thank you, Captain. H'm. But the instructions do insist that the beasts are to be confined to their cages. On the other hand—and our lawyers when the case is brought to court will stress the point—there is no reason given for this injunction." Wendover was oddly embarrassed as he continued. "I have to ask you a personal question, Captain. At the time when the brutes attacked you, were you ... er ... masturbating? I can imagine what it must be like in a ship such as yours, with no company, no female company especially...."

Grimes's prominent ears reddened. "No. I was not. Not consciously. But I was having a remarkably vivid erotic dream...."

"That adds up," said Wendover. "Before I got this job I was Master in Cluster Lines. Their ships maintain a fairly regular service to and from Pangst. After what happened aboard *Cluster Queen* the company has refused to carry *lerrigans*...."

"So Cluster Line personnel didn't keep to the book any more than I did," said Grimes.

"They didn't, Captain. Of course, *lerrigans* are, to a certain degree, telepaths. They hate being confined to cages. They ... broadcast the desire to be let out, to be given the run of the ship, to be petted and cuddled. And spacemen are fond of animals more often than not. Normally there would be no risk—were it not for the *lerrigans'* peculiar sexual makeup. They are stimulated sexually when other animals in their vicinity are stimuated sexually. The Cluster Line ships carry mixed crews. There are always ... liaisons between male and femal officers." Then, disapprovingly, "Even, at times, between males and males and females and females. Be that as it may, you can imagine the effect upon already erotically inclined telepathic beasts...."

He pursed his lips disapprovingly.

"All right," said Grimes. "They were stimulated while I was dreaming. They even ... joined in the dream. But why did they attack me?"

"Because," said Wendover, "to them the killing of another life form, a sexually stimulated life form, is essential before they, themselves, can copulate. Don't ask me why, or how. I'm only a spaceman, not a xenobiologist. All that I know is that I was Master of *Cluster Queen* when I was awakened—when the whole ship was awakened—by the screams from the Third Officer's cabin. When we burst in it was too late. He was dying, shockingly mutilated. His companion, the Purser, was a little luckier. The plastic surgeons were able to rebuild her right breast but psychologically she must have been scarred for life. But what sticks in my memory, even now, is those two obscene, blood spattered beasts unconcernedly doing what they were doing in the corner. I don't think that they knew it when the Chief Engineer battered in the head of first one and then the other with a heavy wrench. . . ."

Remembering his own experience Grimes felt sick.

"Of course," Wendover went on, "they—the consignors and the consignees—will claim that after the *Cluster Queen* affair, and one or two others, not as bad but bad enough, the odd behavior of the *lerrigans* under certain conditions must have been common knowledge among spacemen. Among *merchant* spacemen, yes. But your background, I understand, is Federation Survey Service and I don't suppose that you have, in your ship's library, a copy of Deitweller's *The Carriage Of Exotic Flora And Fauna.* . . ."

"I haven't," admitted Grimes. "I relied upon the *Encyclopedia Galactica.* If I specialized in the carriage of obscure, dead politicians that book would be very useful."

"Ha, ha." Captain Wendover permitted himself a dry chuckle. "And now, Captain Grimes, you must excuse me. There's the problem of compensation for the Third Officer of *Epsilon Draconis*—he had to get himself involved in a rather nasty accident last night. So if you call in here tomorrow morning I'll have our legal eagles —Pendlebury, Worrigan and Pendlebury—here to talk things over with you."

"And when should the case come up, Captain?" asked Grimes.

"I'm a spaceman, not a lawyer, Captain. But as you should know the legal gentry are never in a hurry."

"But my ship's under arrest and the airlock door's been sealed. The only money I have is the Letter of

Credit in my notecase and I have to eat and pay my hotel bill. . . ."

"H'm. I could get you away as Third Officer in the *Epilectic Dragon*—but that would mean that you would not be present in court when the case comes up. Legally that would be in order—I think. After all, your ship is a fine security. . . ."

"I'd sooner stick around," said Grimes. "*If* my ship's going to be sold to pay my bills and fines I want to be among those present."

"Would you be interested in a ship-keeping job, Captain? *Bronson Star's* in parking orbit—it's cheaper than paying port dues—and old Captain Pinner's screaming for a relief. He recently retired out of Trans-Galactic Clippers and he's used to the social life of big passenger ships. But *Bronson Star* would suit you. You're used to being all by yourself in space."

"Not all the time," said Grimes. "But I need the money."

"So does old Captain Pinner. But he decided that he needed company more."

Chapter 3

Bronson Star was the flagship (the only ship) of the Interstellar Shipping Corporation of Bronsonia. She had started her working life as the Interstellar Transport Commission's *Epsilon Argo*. When obsolescent she had been put up for sale—at a time when the Bronsonians were complaining that the standard of the services provided by the major shipping lines to and from their planet was extremely poor. A group of businessmen decided that Bronsonia should have an interstellar merchant fleet of its very own and the sale of shares in this enterprise provided initial working capital. But it had not been an economically viable enterprise. On voyages out of Bronsonia *Bronson Star* barely broke even. On voyages back to her home world, with almost empty holds, she operated at a dead loss.

So the Interstellar Shipping Corporation of Bronsonia swallowed its pride and decommissioned its pet white elephant, having her placed in parking orbit about the planet. There she would remain until such time as a purchaser was found for her. Nonetheless she was too expensive a hunk of hardware to be left entirely unattended; apart from anything else, Lloyd's of London refused to insure her unless she were in the charge of a qualified ship-keeping officer.

The first of these had been the elderly but company-loving Captain Pinner—a typical big passenger shipmaster, Grimes had thought during the comprehensive handing over. The second of these was Grimes. He hoped, as he saw Captain Pinner into the airlock from which he would board the waiting shuttle, that this job would suit him very nicely until his complicated affairs were sorted out. He had quite comfortable living quarters and the life-support systems were working smoothly. The auxiliary hydrogen fusion power generator supplied more than enough current for the requirements of only one man. There was a late model autochef—not nearly so sophisticated as the one aboard *Little Sister* but adequate—and the farm deck had been well maintained; there would be no need to fall back on the algae from the air-purification and sewage-conversion system for nutriment.

After only a week Grimes found that the job was getting him down. He was used to loneliness, especially during his voyages in *Little Sister,* but aboard his own ship there had always been a sense of purpose; he had been going somewhere. Here, in *Bronson Star,* he was going nowhere. As the ship was in an equatorial synchronous orbit this was obvious. She was hanging almost directly over a chain of islands that looked like a sea serpent swimming from east to west—a wedge-shaped head trailed by a string of diminishing wedges. At first he had rather liked the appearance of it but soon was pleased rather than otherwise whenever it was obscured by cloud. That stupid, mythological beast was going nowhere, just as *Bronson Star* was.

Yet time passed. There were his twice daily radio calls to Aerospace Control and, now and again, one to Captain Wendover, the Guild Secretary. Wendover could only tell him that it would be quite some time before the *lerrigan* case came up. He exercised regularly in the ship's gymnasium, an essential routine to one living in Free Fall conditions. He was able to adjust the controls of the autochef so that it would produce meals exactly to his taste; fortunately there was a good supply of spices and other seasonings. He refrained from tinkering with other essential machinery; as long as it was working well he preferred to leave it severely alone. The playmaster in the captain's dayroom was an old model and must have come with the ship when she was purchased from the Commission but it was satis-

factorily operational. The trouble there was that few of
the TriVi programs broadcast from the stations on
Bronsonia appealed to Grimes and the same could be
said of the majority of the spools in the ship's library.
Somebody must have had a passion for the Trust In God
school of playwriting (as Grimes irreverently referred
to it). He would have preferred pornography.

The days—the weeks—went by.

Grimes considered making further modifications to
the autochef so that it could supply him with liquor;
even an old model such as this could have produced a
passable vodka. Yet he held back. In the final analysis
alcohol is no substitute for human company but makes
the addict unfit for such.

Chapter 4

But Grimes got his human company.

He was awakened in the small hours of the morning by the shrilling of the radar alarm. His first thought was that this must be a meteor on a collision course. By the time that he had sealed himself into his spacesuit—even though, to alleviate boredom, he had been carrying out daily emergency drills, the operation took many seconds—he was thinking that the hunk of cosmic debris should have struck by now. A merchant ship's radar does not operate at the same extremely long ranges as the installations aboard fighting vessels. Too, the alarm kept on sounding, which indicated that whatever had set it off was still in close vicinity to *Bronson Star*.

He left his quarters, made for the control room. He went at once to the radar screen. Yes, there was something out there all right, something big. Its range, a mere one kilometer, was neither opening nor closing; its azimuth was not changing. The shuttle from Port Bronson? wondered Grimes. Possibly—but surely Aerospace Control would have warned him that it was coming out to him. He was about to go to the transceiver to call the duty officer at the spaceport when his attention was diverted by a sharp tapping noise, audible even through his helmet. He opened the visor to hear better and to locate the source of the sound. It was coming from one of the viewports.

There was something—no, *somebody*—outside. He could see a helmeted head and, through the transparent faceplate, a pale face. He kicked himself away from the

17

transceiver, fetched up against the viewport rather harder than he had intended. He stared into the eyes of the intruder. It was a woman staring back at him. Her wide mouth moved. She seemed annoyed that he made no reply to what she was saying. He nudged with his chin the on-off button that actuated his own suit radio.

"Help!" she said. "Help! This is urgent. Orbital met. station *Beta*. Explosion. Atmosphere lost. . . ."

One of the orbital met. stations? What the hell was it doing *here?*

"Don't just stand there! Open your airlock door and let us in! Some fool forgot to maintain our suit air bottles. . . ."

"Opening up," said Grimes, pushing himself away from the port and toward the auxiliary machinery control panel. He jabbed a gloved forefinger at the requisite buttons, saw the illuminated PUMP OPERATING sign come on, then PUMP STOPPED, then OUTER DOOR OPEN. The call to Aerospace Control, he decided, could wait until he had the survivors safely on board. He left the control room, hurrying as well as he could in the restrictive space armor, made his way to the head of the axial shaft. Fortunately the elevator cage was already at Captain's Flat level so he did not have to wait for it. Within two minutes he was in the airlock vestibule, watching the illuminated signs over the inner door. At last the OUTER DOOR OPEN was replaced by OUTER DOOR CLOSED. The needle of the airlock pressure gauge began to creep upward from Zero, finally stopped. Before Grimes could thumb the local control button—which, of course, was duplicated inside the chamber—the door began to open. Before it had done so fully a spacesuited figure shuffled through, careful not to break the contact of magnetic soles with the deck.

It was the woman, Grimes realized, with whom he had already talked. He realized, too, that she was holding a heavy pistol of unfamiliar make and that it was pointed at his belly.

Her voice, through his helmet phones, was coldly vicious.

"Don't try anything or I'll blow your guts through your backbone!"

She was followed by three other spacesuited figures. They, too, were armed.

"Take us up to the control room," ordered the woman.

Grimes had no option but to obey.

Only two of the intruders accompanied Grimes into the elevator cage, riding forward (there would be no "up" or "down" until the ship was accelerating) to Control. They told Grimes, menacing him with their weapons, to sit down. He did so, in the chair by the NST transceiver, thinking that he might, given half an opportunity, try to get out a call to Aerospace Control. But the woman anticipated this, fastening his seat belt so that it confined his arms as well as his body.

She asked, "Is this atmosphere breathable?"

He said, "Yes."

"Then why the hell are you wearing a spacesuit?"

"I was awakened by the radar alarm. I thought that it might be a meteor and that the ship might be holed."

"The alarm? It's not sounding now."

It wasn't. The craft that had set it off must now be drifting away from *Bronson Star,* Grimes thought.

"And the air is good, you say? There's just one way of finding out."

But her hands went not to her own helmet but to Grimes's, twisted, lifted. "Thank you," said Grimes, not overly sarcastically. The ship's atmosphere was better than that inside his suit.

"He hasn't died," said the woman, "so it must be all right."

She took off her own headpiece. Her companion followed suit. Grimes looked at the skyjackers curiously. The woman's face was thin, with fine bone structure, with eyes so deep a blue as to be almost black. Her glossy brown hair was swept back to a coil at the nape

of her neck. Her mouth was wide, full lipped, palely
pink in contrast to the deep tan of her skin. The man
could have sat as a model for one of the more decadent
Roman emperors. Greasy black ringlets framed a fleshy
face, with jutting nose over a petulant mouth.

She said, "We are taking your ship. If you cooperate
you will live."

"For the time being," said the man nastily.

Grimes said nothing.

"Has the cat got your tongue?" she asked.

He decided that he had better say something. In any
case he wanted to find out what this was all about.

"Cooperate?" he queried. "How?"

"You know this ship," she said. "We don't. Furthermore—I'll be frank—our navigator got himself killed
when we took over the met. satellite. . . ." She laughed.
"We're all of us spacepersons, of a sort—but met. wall-
ahs. Orbital flights only, apart from Hodge. . . ."

"Hodge?"

"You'll meet him. He's served as engineer in deep-
space ships. He's checking up now. . . ."

A voice came from the intercom speaker. "Hodge to
Lania. Main hydrogen fusion power generator oper-
ating. Inertial and Mannschenn Drives on Stand By.
She's all yours. You'd better get her the hell out of here
before the Aerospace Control boys realize that Station
Beta's not where she's supposed to be."

"Take her away," ordered Lania, addressing Grimes,
making a threatening gesture with her gun hand. Her
companions also displayed their weapons menacingly.

"If I'm dead," said Grimes reasonably, "I shan't be
able to take this ship anywhere."

"If you're dead," she said, "you're dead. Period. It's
quite permanent, you know. Are you going to play
along or not?"

"I'll play," muttered Grimes. "But you have to
release me first."

"Cover him, Paul," she said to her companion, handing him her own pistol. She unsnapped the catch of
Grimes's seat belt, standing to one side so as to leave

a clear field of fire for the guns. Then she stepped smartly back and retrieved her own weapon.

"I have to sit in the command chair," said Grimes.

"Then sit in the command chair. We'll be sitting behind you. We're not such fools as to remain standing while you're sitting trajectory."

"Where do you want to go?" asked Grimes.

"Just get us out of here, fast, the way she's heading now. Mannschenn Drive as soon as you can so that we can't be picked up by Aerospace Control's radar. We'll set trajectory properly later."

Grimes went through the familiar routine. He almost enjoyed it, this awakening of a slumbering ship, this breaking out and away from that deadly dull parking orbit. He would have enjoyed it had he not been acting under duress. There was the arhythmic cacaphony of the inertial drive and. with the acceleration, blessed gravity again after the weeks of Free Fall. The ship was now headed, he saw, looking up through the transparency of the forward viewport, for the bright star that was the major luminary of the constellation called, by the Bronsonians, the Hobbit. He did not suppose that any world revolving about that primary would be the destination but it was as good a target star as any for the time being.

He cut the inertial drive. Would the sudden return to weightless conditions give him the opprtunity to do something, anything? From behind him he heard the tense whisper, "Watch it, Grimes! Watch it. We have you covered." He sighed, audibly. He said, "Stand by Mannschenn Drive, for temporal disorientation."

There was the almost inaudible humming, a vibration rather than a sound, as the gyroscopes began to spin, a low hum that gradually heightened its pitch to a thin, high whine. As always, Grimes visualized that complexity of gleaming rotors, spinning, tumbling, precessing, warping the Continuum about the ship and all aboard her. Perspective was disorted and colors sagged down the spectrum. There was the usual dizziness, the faint nausea—and then inside the ship all was normal once more but outside, seen through the view-ports the stars were no longer hard, diamond-sharp points of light but writhing, iridiscent nebulosities. Still in view, just abaft the beam, was Bronsonia, no longer a sphere but a sluggishly pulsating ellipsoid.

Grimes restarted the inertial drive and it dwindled to invisibility.

Chapter 5

Hodge and his companion came up to Control.

They were spacesuited still but with the faceplates of their helmets open, their heavy gauntlets tucked into their belts. Hodge was a little man with coarse, dark hair growing low on his forehead, with muddy brown eyes under thick brows, a bulbous nose and a mouth that was little more than a wrinkle in the deeply tanned skin of his face over a receding chin. *The Last of the Neanderthalers,* thought Grimes. He remembered them —his mind was a junk room littered with scraps of un-related knowledge—reading somewhere that Neander-thal Man had been a technician superior to the more conventionally human Cro-Magnards.

The person with Hodge was also of less than average height. The lustrous hair that framed her face was golden with a reddish tint. Unusual for a blonde, she was brown-eyed. Her face was not quite chubby, her nose was slightly uptilted, her scarlet-lipped mouth was generous. Grimes thought—even now he could regard an attractive woman with interest—*A lovely dollop of trollop.* And what was she doing in this galley?

Hodge growled, "It's all systems Go."

"All systems have gone," commented Lania. "Or didn't you notice? And what about the life-support sys-tems, Susie? That's your department."

"We'll not starve," replied the small blonde. Her voice, a rich contralto, was not the childish soprano that Grimes had expected. "We may not live like kings . . ." and why, Grimes wondered, should Hodge laugh,

23

should the other male skyjacker scowl? ". . . but we'll not go hungry or thirsty or asphyxiate."

"After all," contributed Grimes, "*I* didn't."

"Shut up, you!" snapped Lania. She addressed the others, "I suggest, Paul, that we continue on this trajectory until we've gotten ourselves organized. We have to arrange accommodation for ourselves to begin with. So, Hodge, I'd like you to fit a lock on the door of the Third Officer's cabin that can be operated only from the outside. *Captain* Grimes . . ." so she knew his name . . . "will shift his things—such things as we allow him to keep, that is—to that accommodation. Paul and I will occupy the Master's suite. You, Hodge, should be happy in the Chief Engineer's quarters. And you, Susie, can take up residence in the Purser's cabin. So, Grimes, get moving!"

Grimes didn't like it; somehow he resented this demotion accommodationwise even more than the seizure of the ship. It was many a long year since he had occupied a junior officer's cabin. But there was no arguing with the pistols that were pointing at him.

He unsnapped the buckle of his seat belt, rose from his chair and walked slowly to the hatch that gave access to the deck below Control. The others followed him but the engineer, Hodge, did not accompany them into the accommodation that Grimes had come to regard as a sort of home.

Clothing he would need, thought Grimes, and toilet gear, and pipe and tobacco. And, if he were to be incarcerated, reading matter; from a very early age he had been addicted to the printed word.

"Take off your spacesuit, Grimes," ordered Lania. "Leave it here."

"But. . . ."

"Do as I say. Do you think that we want you escaping and clambering around the outside of the ship?"

Grimes had donned the protective garment hastily when the alarm sounded, had not taken time to put on the longjohns that were the usual underwear with space armor. Although he had always regarded the fantastically persistent nudity taboo as absurd, he was reluctant to disrobe; nakedness on a sunny beach among fellow nudists is altogether different from being unclothed surrounded by hostile, fully dressed, armed strangers. But he had no option but to do as he was told. He stripped. Lania looked at him coldly, almost contemptuously. Susie regarded him with frank appraisal. He felt his prominent ears reddening with embarrassment. The flush spread to his face, down over his body.

He asked, with what dignity he could muster, "Can I dress now?"

"Your watch," demanded Lania. "You'll know *nothing,* not even the time, except when we require your services."

He loosened the wrist strap, dropped the instrument on top of the discarded spacesuit.

Lania said, "Susie, get a shirt and shorts out of his wardrobe. Make sure that there's nothing in the pockets."

The other woman obeyed, handing the garments to Grimes. He dressed hastily.

"Toilet gear?" he asked.

"Permitted," said Lania. "Get it out of the bathroom for him, Susie."

"My pipe. . . . Tobacco. . . ."

"Yes. You can get that rubbish out of here; neither of us smokes. But no lighter or matches or whatever you use for ignition."

"But. . . ."

"You heard me. Fire is a weapon."

Grimes decided not to argue. He said, "If I'm to be imprisoned for most of this voyage I'd like some books."

"We haven't spared your life, Grimes, so that you can catch up on your back reading."

Susie intervened. "He won't be navigating *all* the time. Let him have something to keep his mind occupied."

"Oh, all right. Give him his bedtime stories."

Grimes took two volumes from the bookcase, both

of them novels left by his predecessor and which he had never gotten around to reading.

"All right," snapped Lania. "Enough. Get him out of here."

Clutching his pitifully few possessions he left what were no longer his own quarters, was hustled down a deck to the officers' flat. The Third Officer's cabin had been prepared for his occupancy. Hodge had found a combination padlock in the engine-room stores, had welded a hasp and staple to the door and its frame. The main consideration, however, had been security rather than comfort. There was no bed linen on the bunk and the deckhead light tube was defective. The chair by the desk looked decidedly rickety. The settee cushion cover was torn. The only touch of color was a ship-chandler's calendar, useless for telling the date save on its planet of origin, depicting in startling, three-dimensional color a young lady proudly displaying her supernormal mammary development.

"Stay here until we want you," ordered Lania.

When the door shut after her, when Grimes heard the sharp click of the padlock snapping shut, he knew that all he could do was just that.

He made a thorough search of his new quarters. The toilet facilities, he was relieved to find, were operational although very cramped after the ones that he had become accustomed to. In one of the desk drawers were a few tattered magazines; evidently the Third Mate of *Bronson Star*—whoever he was and whatever he was doing now—had been a devotee of Hard Downbeat. Grimes permitted himself a sneer; he had never understood how that derivation from the ancient Portuguese *fado* had achieved such popularity. Then, in another drawer, he found a treasure—a rechargeable electric lighter. He pressed the stud and the ignition element at the end of the little cylinder glowed into incandescence. He made no attempt to fight temptation; after all he had become accustomed, over the years, to starting his day with a cup of coffee and a pipe of tobacco. This day had started some considerable time ago and it didn't look as though there were going to be any coffee but his pipe would be better than nothing. It was an aid to thinking.

He went through to the tiny bathroom, made sure that the exhaust fan was functioning, then lit up. He started to think about his predicament. He realized, with something of a shock, that there was something that he should have brought with him into what was to be his prison cell. This was a solidograph of Maggie Lazenby, a very special one, made on her home world, Arcadia. This planet being blessed with a subtropical climate almost from pole to pole, its inhabitants went about naked most of the time and would no more have dreamed of wearing a costume on the beach than under the shower in the bathroom. . . . The solidograph was in one of the drawers of the wardrobe; Grimes had placed it there rather than have it drifting around, with the possibility of damage, while the ship was in free fall. Perhaps, he thought, it would stay there. Perhaps Lania and Paul would not find it. He hated the idea of that fat slob holding that three-dimensional portrait of the naked Maggie in his greasy hands. . . .

Perhaps if he asked. . . .

But if he did Lania and Paul would know of its existence.

He decided that he might as well have a shower, freshen up. He stripped, stood in the little cubicle to be sprayed with hot water and detergent. He applied depilatory cream to his face, rinsed, then dried off under the warm air blast.

Naked, he padded through into the cabin just as the outer door opened, admitting Susie. Hodge, carrying the inevitable pistol, was behind her. Once again Grimes was at a disadvantage but, somehow, did not feel the same embarrassment that he had felt before. Susie smiled sweetly. Hodge grinned, displaying strong, yellow teeth, aimed his pistol where it would do maximum if not immediately lethal damage.

Susie said, "You're wanted in Control. You can
come as you are if you wish."

He said briefly, "I'll dress."

As he pulled on his shorts and shirt he noticed that
she and Hodge were no longer wearing spacesuits but
were in a uniform that was strange to him. They must
have brought a change of clothing with them from the
meteorological satellite—but the devices on the shoulder
boards of their shirts had no connection with Bronsonian meteorology or meteorology in general. Silver stars?
Common enough, perhaps; people were wearing stars
as marks of rank long, long before the first clumsy
rocket soared out and away from old Earth. But golden
crowns? There was no monarchy on Bronsonia. Surely,
thought Grimes, these people could not be refugees from
the Waverley Royal Mail. . . .

Then, with Susie and Hodge bringing up the rear, he
made his way to the control room.

Chapter 6

Lania and Paul were also wearing the strange uniform although theirs was black and not, as in the case of Susie and Hodge, slate grey, but they wore long trousers and not shorts and high-necked blouses rather than shirts. And Paul's shoulder boards bore veritable clusters of silver stars under the golden crowns and although Lania's were not so profusely star-spangled each one carried a not-so-minor constellation.

"Be seated, Grimes," ordered Lania.

Sullenly Grimes complied.

"Now," she went on, "we'll find out if you can navigate. I'll tell you where I want you to take this rustbucket. . . ."

Grimes said nothing but he must have looked as though he were thinking.

"Be careful, Grimes. If the thought has flickered across your tiny mind that you can turn the ship around and head back for Bronsonia, forget it. We may not be navigators—but even we would be aware of such a large alteration of trajectory. And even if we should somehow fail to notice what you did we would know as soon as we got there. And then. . . ."

She jerked her pistol suggestively.

You're enjoying this, thought Grimes. *You female-chauvinist bitch. . . .*

"Where to?" he asked.

"In future," she told him, "please address me as Highness."

He stared at her. She was quite serious although he noticed Susie and Hodge exchange a sardonic glance.

29

Her . . . husband? lover? did not seem to find what she had said at all out of the ordinary, however, merely maintained his pose of superior boredom.

"Where to, Highness?" repeated Grimes.

"Porlock."

"I shall have to take a fix, Highness, and then I have to set up the chart and identify the Porlock sun. . . ."

"We have you along, Grimes, just to handle such sordid details."

He got up from his chair, went to the Carlotti transceiver. He wondered briefly if he would be able to push out a message over the interstellar communications system but realized, almost at once, that this would be impossible. Somebody—Hodge, presumably—had removed vital components. The equipment was now a receiver only, although capable of direction finding. He returned to the chart tank, ran up a dead-reckoning trajectory from Bronsonia, noted which three Carlotti Beacon stations in relatively nearby space were most advantageously situated with reference to the ship. He took his bearings, saw that the three filaments of luminescence intersected very close indeed to his estimated position. (If they had not done so there would have been something somewhere seriously wrong.) He set up an extrapolated trajectory from the fix.

Now, Porlock. . . .

A navigator he might be but he had no idea as to where in the universe *it* might be although he recalled the circumstances of its naming, the story being one of the legends of the Survey Service. One of the old-time Commodores, a man whose name was Coleridge and who claimed descent from that poet, had been interrupted while he was doing something important by a call from the control room of his ship to tell him that the sun which the vessel was approaching had at least one habitable planet in orbit. Accounts varied as to what the "something important" was. The one generally accepted was that he was on the point of beating down the stubborn resistance of one of the female scientists carried on the exploratory expedition. Another was that he, following in the footsteps of his illustrious ancestor, was in the throes of composing a piece of poetry that would ensure for him literary immortality. In either case —or in any of the other hypothetical cases—Porlock was the obvious name for the body responsible for the interruption.

Porlock. . . .

The ship's navigational data bank flashed the co-ordinates onto the screen almost immediately. Grimes had to reduce the scale of the chart tank so as to include the Porlock sun. He discovered then that there was no convenient target star. The first adjustment of trajectory, therefore, must be made on instruments only. This was no more than a minor inconvenience.

Resuming his command seat, he shut down inertial and Mannschenn drives while the others watched him intently, their pistols ready. He turned the ship on her axes around the directional gyroscopes. He restarted the inertial drive and then the space-time-twisting Mann-schenn. Sometimes, on such occasions, there were flash-es of déjà vu to accompany the spatial and temporal disorientation—but this time (as far as Grimes was concerned) there was only the discomfort of mild nausea. The chilling thought came to him that perhaps he had no future.

But he knew that he must continue to cooperate until such time—if ever—as he had a chance, however faint, to escape.

Lania got up from her chair to look into the chart tank, then stared out and up through the viewports at the stars, mere vague nebulosities as seen in the warped continuum engendered by the ever-precessing rotors of the Drive. She looked away hastily, back into the tank.

She said accusingly, "That . . . that extrapolated trajectory or whatever you call it misses the Porlock sun by light years!"

"Allowance for galactic drift," he told her.

"Haven't you forgotten something?" she asked coldly.

It took him some little time to realize what she was driving at. Then, "Allowance for galactic drift, Highness," he said, hating himself for according her that title.

"Hodge and Susie," she ordered, "take him back to his kennel." Then, "Oh, before you tear yourself away from us, Grimes, what is our estimated time of arrival?"

"At our present precession rate and at an acceleration of one gravity just thirty standard days, Highness."

She made no acknowledgment, voiced neither approval nor disapproval, saying only, "Take him back to his kennel."

Chapter 7

Grimes missed his watch. And there was no bulkhead clock in the Third Officer's cabin; her original owners, the Interstellar Transport Commission, were parsimonious in some respects, considering that only departmental heads were entitled to certain "luxuries."

But time would pass whether or not he possessed the mechanical means of recording its passage. One way of passing time is to sit and think. Grimes went through to the bathroom to do his sitting and thinking; he could smoke his pipe in there without its becoming obvious to anybody entering the cabin that he had found the means of lighting the thing.

He sat and he thought.

He thought about the skyjackers. The man called Paul was wearing the most gold and silver braid so, presumably, was the leader. But Lania, with fewer stars and smaller crowns on her shoulder boards, was the one giving all the orders—leader *de facto* if not *de jure*. The situation, perhaps, was analogous to that obtaining when a rather ineffectual Captain is overshadowed by a tough, dynamic First Lieutenant or Chief Mate or whatever.

Hodge? Just another engineer, no matter where he came from or whose badges he was wearing.

Susie? Her like could be found in many spaceships, both naval and mercantile. She was no more (and no less) than a spacefaring hotel manager.

All four of the skyjackers, it seemed, had been in the employ of the Bronsonian Meteorological Service, crewpersons aboard Station *Beta*. How big a crew did those artificial satellites carry? Grimes didn't know. But there must have been a mutiny, during which one of the skyjackers, the navigator of the party, had been killed. Somebody else—possibly the captain, with the muzzle of a pistol pressing into the back of his neck—had driven *Beta* out of her circumpolar orbit into one intersecting that of *Bronson Star*.

And this "Highness" business. . . .

Grimes had known Highnesses and Excellencies and the like and was prepared to admit that Lania and Paul did have about them something of that aura which distinguishes members of hereditary aristocracy from the common herd. He knew what it was, of course. It was no more than plain arrogance; if you have it drummed into you from birth on that you are better than those in whose veins blue blood does not flow you will end up really believing it.

But what had a Highness been doing as a crewwoman aboard an orbital spacecraft? A met. observatory owned by a planet state whose elected ruler bore the proud title of First People's Minister, not First Peoples' Minister. . . . Grimes allowed himself a break to enjoy the semantic subtlety.

He heard the cabin door open, voices.

(Didn't these people ever knock?)

He got up, knocked his pipe out into the toilet bowl (the one operational only during acceleration), flushed. He put the pipe into his pocket, came through into the cabin.

Susie said brightly, "Oh, there you are. Making room for breakfast?"

Hodge, behind her, grinned.

"Breakfast?" queried Grimes, looking at the tray that she set down on his desk. He was hungry, but a bowl of stew, however savory, did not seem right, somehow, for the first meal of the day.

"Or lunch, or dinner. Take your pick. But it has to be something that you can eat out of a soft, plastic bowl with a soft, plastic spoon. Her Highness's orders."

"Her Highness?"

"That's what we all have to call her now. And Paul, of course, is His Highness.

"But Bronsonia's a sort of republic."

"And where we came from wasn't. Or, to be more exact, where our parents came from."

"Porlock?" wondered Grimes. "But Porlock's a republic too—unless it's changed since I did my last Recent Galactic History course."

"May as well tell him, Susie," said Hodge. "He can listen while he's eating. I've more important things to do than play at being your armed escort."

"All right," said the girl. "Get dug into your tucker and listen. Our parents were refugees from Dunlevin. You may recall from your history courses that Dunlevin *was* a monarchy. Paul's father *was* the Crown Prince; he was one of the few members of the royal family who got away in the royal yacht. Lania's parents were the Duke and Duchess of Barstow, who also escaped. Hodge's father was an officer in the Royal Dunlevin Navy. My father was too, Paymaster Commander of the yacht.

"Wallis, who *should* have been our navigator on this caper, was the son of Commodore Wallis, a loyalist officer. As a matter of fact he—young Wallis, that is—was Third Mate of this ship before he entered the met. service. . . ."

Grimes worked his way through the plate of stew while she was talking. It wasn't too bad, although he, had he been cooking, would have programmed the autochef to be more generous with the seasonings. And the mug of coffee that came with the meal was deficient in sweetening.

Susie's story was interesting. He remembered, now, reading about the revolution on Dunlevin. The ruling house on that planet had not been at all popular and, as Dunlevin was of little strategic importance, had not been propped up by Federation weaponry. Even so the Popular Front had not enjoyed a walkover, mainly because the Royalists had been given support—arms and "volunteers"—by the Duchy of Waldegren. The Interstellar Federation, albeit reluctantly, had imposed a blockade on Dunlevin. The Federation did not like the Popular Front but liked Waldegren even less. And it was Federation presence that prevented too enthusiastic a massacre when the last Royalist stronghold fell; shiploads of refugees made their escape under the guns of the blockading Survey Service fleet.

Some of those refugees, obviously, had found haven on Bronsonia.

"So," said Grimes after he had swallowed the last spoonful, "you people hope to mount a counterrevolution. . . . I'm sorry to be a wet blanket—but you haven't the hope of a snowball in hell. This rustbucket isn't a warship, you know. Or hadn't you noticed?"

"Any ship," she told him sweetly, "is a potential troop transport. And any merchant vessel is a potential auxiliary cruiser. It's rather a pity, Grimes, that we shall be leaving you on Porlock. We could have used your Survey Service expertise."

He said, "I'm not a mercenary."

She said, "But certain episodes in your past career indicate that you're willing to fight on the right side."

He said, "The *right* side isn't necessarily the right side."

"Ha. Ha bloody ha. If you've ever lived under a left-wing tyranny you'd be talking differently."

"Have you ever lived under a left-wing tyranny, Susie?"

"No. But we know how things are on Dunlevin."

"Do you?"

"Yes!" she snapped. "Have you finished your meal?" She snatched the tray off the desk. "We'll leave you now. You'll be told when you're required again."

"There should be at least a once-daily check of position," said Grimes.

"You people," she told him scornfully, "are always trying to kid us, those of us who aren't members of the Grand Lodge of Navigators, that you're indispensible."

And with those parting words she left him.

Chapter 8

The voyage wore on.

It was a voyage such as Grimes had never experienced before, such as he hoped that he would never experience again. He was able to keep track of the passage of objective time only because, at irregular intervals, he was taken up to the control room to check the ship's position. Finally he had target sun, the Porlock primary, and knew, with a combination of relief and apprehension, that the passage was almost over. Until Lania was able to replace him with a navigator who was one of her own people he was safe. Once his services were no longer required would he be set free on Porlock? And if he were, how would he make his way back from that planet to Bronsonia? And would he find *Little Sister* still there? Would she have been sold to pay his various debts and fines?

The only one of the skyjackers who was at all friendly was Susie. Paul was becoming more and more the Crown Prince—the King, rather—and Lania a sort of hybrid, a cross between Queen and Grand Vizier. And Hodge, Grimes felt, was taking sadistic delight in the spectacle of a space captain at the receiving end of orders.

Susie's friendliness was due, partly, to missionary zeal. But whom was she trying to convince—herself or Grimes? He judged that she was beginning to regret having become involved in this enterprise, that she was realizing, although she would hate to admit it, that she had far more in common with Grimes, the apolitical outsider, than with her dedicated companions.

Meanwhile she soon discovered that he was smoking in the cabin that was also his prison. Not only did she turn a blind eye—or insensitive nose—but actually brought him more tobacco from the ship's stores when his own ran out. And she gave him a chess set, and reading matter. Most of this latter consisted of propaganda magazines; it seemed that there was quite a colony of refugees from Dunlevin on Bronsonia.

Grimes rather doubted that the accounts of life on Dunlevin, as printed in these journals, were altogether accurate. He did know, from his reading of recent history during his Survey Service days, that life on that world had been far from pleasant for the common people during the monarchy. They must have welcomed the transition of power from kings to commissars. And were the commissars as bad as the kings had been? Grimes doubted it. Dunlevin aristocracy and royalty were descended from the notorious Free Brotherhood, pirates who, as a prelude to the erection of a facade of respectability, had taken over a newly colonized planet, virtually enslaving its inhabitants.

He argued with Susie during his meal times. It passed the time although it was all rather pointless; neither of them possessed first-hand knowledge of conditions on Dunlevin.

He asked her, "Why should you, an attractive girl who had a secure and reasonably happy future on Bronsonia—where you were born—throw away everything to play a part in this—*your* word, Susie—caper?"

She was frank with him.

"Partly," she admitted, "because of the way that I was brought up. Father—even though he manages a restaurant—is still very much the Royal Dunlevin Navy officer. Mother—customers refer to her as the Duchess—is still the aristocrat. They believe, sincerely, that it is my duty to help to restore the House of Carling to the throne and to destroy the socialist usurpers. . . ."

"While they stay put in their hash house, raking in the profits."

"They're no longer young, Captain. And they have contributed, substantially, to the Restoration Fund."

"And so," said Grimes, "when Their Royal Highnesses raise a tattered banner and beat a battered drum your parents are proud and happy to see their darling daughter falling into step, risking *her* neck. . . ."

"They are proud. Of course they're proud."

"But how come there're so few of you? Just Paul and Lania and Hodge and yourself—and whoever it was that got himself killed in the met. satellite?"

"Because we were the only ones able to be in the right place at the right time to seize this ship. And it took lots of undercover organizing to get us all aboard *Beta* at the same time. But on Porlock. . . ."

"That's enough yapping," grumbled Hodge. "Come on, Susie. I've work to do, even if some other people haven't."

Chapter 9

Grimes brought *Bronson Star* down to Porlock.

He sat in the control room, with Their Royal Highnesses and Susie in other chairs so situated that they could cover him with their pistols without risk of shooting each other. He told them that if they did kill him they, in all probability, would die too. Lania told him that even she knew enough to use the inertial drive to reverse the vessel's fall. He said that the NST transceiver should be used to request permission from Aerospace Control to make entry. She told him that this was not only unnecessary but impossible since the Aerospace Controllers were on strike—a stoppage, thought Grimes, conveniently timed to coincide with *Bronson Star's* planetfall. Doubtless a coded message had been sent to somebody by means of the Carlotti Deep Space radio.

In any case the landing was not to be made at Port Coleridge. Grimes had been supplied with charts and told that he was to set the ship down at the point indicated at precisely 2000 local time for that locality. (Porlock, like many worlds with a period of rotation less than that of Earth, found it convenient to adopt a twenty-hour day.) The set-down site, ringed in red on the map, was in one of the deserts that occupied most of the land space of the southern continent of this world. It was, Grimes estimated, at least five hundred Porlock miles (one thousand kilometers) from the nearest town. Noisy as the inertial drive inevitably is, the midnight landing should go unheard in any center of population.

Grimes always enjoyed ship handling and, in spite of the circustances, he found pleasure in this test of his skill. There was no Aerospace Control to keep him informed as to what the wind was doing at the various levels of the atmosphere. Even if *Bronson Star* had been equipped with sounding rockets he would not have been allowed to use them. But there was a beacon, a bright red light visible only from above, that he was able to pick up from a great altitude; fortunately it was a cloudless night.

That ruddy spark, as soon as he had it in the sternvision screen, allowed him to estimate drift, which was easily compensated for by lateral thrust although requiring frequent adjustment. Grimes quite forgot that he was acting under duress except when Paul, superciliously obnoxious, remarked that professional spacemen always seem to suffer from the delusion that their ships are made of glass.

The beacon light grew brighter and brighter, so much so that Grimes was obliged to reduce the brilliance of the screen. He watched the radar altimeter and when there were only one hundred and fifty meters to go allowed the target to drift away from the center of the bull's-eye sight.

"Watch it, Grimes!" ordered Lania sharply. "Watch your aim!"

He said, "I'm looking after your property, or somebody's property, Highness. Those laser beacons are quite expensive, you know . . ."

"You're not paying for it!" she snapped but refrained from any further interference.

One hundred. . . . Fifty. . . . Grimes increased vertical thrust to slow the rate of descent. *Forty. . . . Thirty. . . . Bronson Star* was drifting down like a huge balloon with barely negative buoyancy. *Five. . . . Four. . . . Three. . . . Two. . . . One. . . .*

And they were down, with hardly a jar. Grimes stopped the drive and the ship sighed as she adjusted her great weight within the cradle of her tripedal landing gear. The clinometer indicated that she was only a fraction of a degree off the vertical.

Grimes felt for his pipe then remembered that he had left it in his cabin. In any case Their Royal Highnesses would not have tolerated smoking in their presence.

He said, "We're here."

"A blinding glimpse of the obvious, Grimes," said Lania.

"They're waiting for us, Highness," said Susie.

"It would be strange if they were not, girl. Mortdale is a good organizer."

Grimes asked, "May I ring off the engines, Highness?"

"No. Leave everything on Stand By. We just might have to—what is the expression?—get upstairs in a hurry. So remain at your controls."

Without leaving his chair Grimes was able to look out through the wide viewports. There was activity outside the ship—dark shapes in the darkness, flashing lights, the occasional flashing reflection from bright metal.

Susie," ordered Lania, "go down to the airlock to receive General Mortdale. You should recognize him from his photographs and you have the password."

"Yes, Highness."

Susie vanished down the hatch.

Grimes started to ask, "Shall I be . . . ?"

"Speak when you're spoken to," he was told.

Eventually Susie returned.

She was accompanied by three men, clad in drab, insignialess coveralls. Their leader—Mortdale?—was small, compact, terrier-like, with a stubble of gray hair and a close-cropped moustache. Grimes had known officers like him in the Federation Survey Service Marines, had never cared for them. Terriers—stupidly pugnacious at best, vicious at worst—were not his favorite dogs. The other two were taller than their leader. One had yellow hair, the other was bald but they could almost have been twins. Looking at their hard, reckless faces Grimes categorized them as bad bastards.

Mortdale drew himself to attention, so sharply that Grimes was surprised not to hear vertebrae cracking. "Highness!" he snapped.

"General," acknowledged Paul with a languid nod of his head.

"May I present Major Briggs and Captain Polanski?"

The two men bowed stiffly.

"Captain Polanski, I suppose," said Paul, "is the spaceman who will be taking over from our unwilling ... chauffeur."

"No, Highness. The captain is a member of my staff."

"Then may I suggest, General, that you get your qualified spaceman aboard as soon as possible? There are the holds to convert into troop accommodation, the stores and the weapons to load, the troops to embark. This work must be supervised."

"It can be supervised by an army officer, Highness," said Mortdale.

"What about the man you were supposed to have for us?" demand Lania sharply.

"Him?" The general's voice was contemptuous. "He backed out. There was some star tramp here short of an officer and so he got himself signed on as Third Mate without letting me know. By this time he's halfway to Ultimo."

"I would have expected you to exercise better control over your people, General Mortdale," said Lania coldly. "Thanks to your negligence the success of the operation has been jeopardized. The work of conversion, the loading, the embarkation must inevitably be delayed. It will not be long before the planetary authorities realize that something odd is going on out here in the desert."

"The World Manager and his ministers are sympathetic to our cause, Highness. They hope for a favorable trade agreement with the new government on Dunlevin. . . ."

"And who gave *you* the authority to negotiate such deals?" demanded Paul hotly. "Who. . . ."

Lania silenced him with an imperious wave of her hand.

"And as I have already said, Highness," went on the general, "my officers can oversee the work at least as well as any spaceman. As for the lift-off and the navigation to Dunlevin . . ." Grimes realized that Mortdale's rather mad, yellow eyes were staring directly at him . . . *"he,* whoever he is, got you here. He must be competent. He can take us away from here."

"He will do as he's told," said Lania, "if he values his health."

Grimes said, "I understood that I was to be released on this world. Highness."

"Did you?" Then, to Mortdale, "Have your officers put him back in his kennel until we need him again. Susie will show them where it is."

Chapter 10

Locked in his cabin once more Grimes stretched out on his bunk. He had never felt so helpless before in his entire life. He listened to the sounds that told him of the work in progress—hammerings, occasional muffled shouts, the rattle of ground vehicles being driven up the loading ramp to the cargo port. He could visualize what was being done; among the courses that he had sat through during his Survey Service career was one dealing with the conversion of commercial vessels to military purposes. If he'd been doing the job, he thought, he would have utilized inflatable troop-deck fittings— but that presupposed the availability of the necessary materials. Failing that, tiers of bunks could be knocked up from timber or fabricated from metal.

He wondered which technique was being used. Although this was not his ship—he had been little more than a caretaker and now was a prisoner—he still felt responsible for her. And, at brief intervals, when handling a lift-off or set-down or when adjusting trajectory, he would be, after a fashion, in actual command.

Susie came in briefly, escorted by one of Mortdale's men. She brought him a packet of sandwiches and a plastic mug of coffee. She said little, was obviously reluctant to speak in front of the stranger.

Grimes enjoyed the light meal; it took a lot to put him off his food. He enjoyed the pipe afterward. While smoking it he tried to think things out. He would have to play along, he decided. Even though he owed no loyalty to the Royal House of Dunlevin he owed none

45

to the Council of Commissars who were that planet's present rulers. Voluntarily he would serve neither. Under duress he would do what he was told until— and that would, indeed, be the sunny Friday—a chance presented itself for him to make his escape.

And meanwhile—what was happening back on Bronsonia? Had his case been brought before the court yet? And if so, how had it gone? Had he lost his ship—*his* ship—the golden *Little Sister?* His worries about his legal affairs did, at least, help to take his mind off his present predicament.

And then, telling himself that there was nothing that he could do about anything at this present moment, he allowed himself to drift into a troubled sleep.

The period of his incarceration passed slowly.

Susie, always accompanied by an armed man, brought him his meals at what seemed to be regular intervals. He asked her how the work of conversion into a troop transport was going. She answered him shortly on each occasion, noncommittally, obviously inhibited by the presence of her escort.

Then, at last, she was able to tell him that lift-off would be as soon as he got himself up to Control. Grimes welcomed this intelligence. Given recreational facilities he did not object to a period of idleness but with no playmaster and no reading matter apart from those two novels (which he had finished long since and that were not worth reading) and the propaganda magazines he was becoming bored.

Paul and Lania were in the control room, as was General Mortdale. The soldier was still wearing his drab coveralls but shoulder straps, bearing the now familiar silver stars and golden crown insignia, had been added.

"Take her up," ordered Lania.

"Where to?" asked Grimes. "Or need I ask? Highness."

She looked at him coldly. "As you said, need you ask? And now, what are you waiting for?"

Grimes said, "First I have to do some checking. Highness."

He looked out of the ports. He saw nothing but darkness. This was to be a midnight lift-off just as it had been a midnight set-down. A glance at the chronometer and a minor conversion calculation confirmed this. He walked to the big panel presenting information regarding the current state of the ship, noted from the indicators that her mass had been considerably increased but not to the extent to place any undue strain upon the inertial drive. He wished that he knew the makeup of this extra weight—how many men, how many armed vehicles, what weapons, what stores? But the question was an academic one. All life-support systems were functioning. Airlock doors were closed.

"Take your time, Grimes," said Lania sarcastically.

"Take your time, Captain," said Mortdale, without irony. "Make sure that everything is as it should be." To Lania he remarked, "A good commander takes nothing for granted, Highness."

"There's one thing that he can take for granted," snapped the Crown Princess. "And that's that he'll get his head blown off if he attempts anything that he shouldn't. All right, Grimes, get us away from here."

Grimes strapped himself into the command chair. He said into the intercom microphone, "All hands stand by for lift-off. Secure all."

"All has been secured," said the general.

The inertial drive muttered irritably and then commenced its arhythmic hammering. The noise, thanks to sonic insulation, was not too loud in either the control room or the accommodation. Grimes wondered if anybody had thought to insulate the cargo holds, which were now troop decks. He rather hoped that this had not been done. It would make him a little happier to know that Paul's and Lania's loyal soldiers would be experiencing a thoroughly uncomfortable passage.

Bronson Star heaved her clumsy bulk off the gibber plain, clawed for the sky. She lifted complainingly. Grimes doubted that the weight of her cargo, animate

and inanimate, had been properly distributed. But the
Commission's Epsilon Class star tramps were sturdy
workhorses and could stand considerable abuse.

She groaned and grumbled into the black, star-
spangled sky. As on the occasion of her landing there
was no communication with Aerospace Control. Grimes
wondered what report, what complaints would be made
by the captain of the big airliner, a dirigible ablaze with
lights, that passed within ten kilometers of the climbing spaceship; even though *Bronson Star* was not ex-
hibiting the regulation illuminations, she would have
shown up as an enormous blip on the aircraft's radar
screen.

She drove through the last, tenuous wisps of atmosphere, out and up, through the Van Allens, established
herself in orbit. Grimes was busy, as was the computer,
presenting him with the cordinates of the target star.
There was Free Fall when the inertial drive was shut
off, centrifugal effects while the directional gyroscopes
when the Mannschenn Drive propagated its artificial,
turned the ship about her axes, temporal disorientation
warped continuum about the vessel. Inertial drive again,
and a comfortable one-gravity acceleration. . . .

"Back to your kennel, Grimes," said Lania.

Chapter 11

Grimes could not help worrying.

Even though he felt nothing but dislike for Paul and Lania and their people—with one possible exception—he still felt responsible for them. He was not the only spaceman aboard the ship—the original skyjackers must have received some sort of training before being employed in orbital vehicles and Hodge had served in deep-space vessels—but he was the only master astronaut. During the voyage from Bronsonia to Porlock he had not been overly concerned; the life-support systems had been required to serve the needs of only five persons. But now. . . . It is axiomatic that the more people there are aboard a ship the more things there are that can go wrong. *Somebody* should be making rounds at regular intervals. *Somebody* should be seeing to it that the departmental heads—Hodge and Susie?—were doing their jobs efficiently. *Somebody* should be inspecting the troop decks to ensure that conditions were reasonably hygienic. In Grimes's experience even marines, for all their spit and polish, could not be trusted to maintain a high standard of personal cleanliness. And these soldiers that the ship was carrying were not marines, were only irregulars although, presumably, General Mortdale had been an officer in the army of Dunlevin prior to the revolution.

Then—*to hell with them,* thought Grimes. After all he was not legally responsible for anything. His name was not on the Register as Master of this ship; he had been employed only as a glorified watchman. He wanted to stay alive himself, of course, but could hardly care

less what happened to his captors. He would be able to
tell, he thought, if there were a dangerous buildup of
carbon dioxide in the atmosphere or if the water-puri-
fication system were not functioning properly. If he
suspected that things were going wrong he would tell
Susie when she brought him his food.

One of the worst features of his incarceration was
never knowing, except on the occasions when he was
brought up to Control for navigation, what the time
was. Sometimes it seemed only minutes between meals,
sometimes far too many hours. He was never sure when
he should be sleeping or reading—not that there was
anything worth reading—or exercising. (He tried to
keep himself in reasonably good condition by push-ups
and sit-ups and toe-touchings, all that he could manage
in his cramped quarters.)

He was having a shower. (It was one way of passing
the time.) He washed his shirt and shorts, hung them
to dry in the warm air blast. He stepped through from
the little bathroom into the not much larger cabin just
as the door opened and Susie stepped in. He glimpsed
Hodge in the alleyway outside as the door shut. He
heard the click of the padlock closing.

He was conscious of his nakedness but he had no
towel to wrap about himself and he was damned if he
was going to put on his wet shorts and shirt for anybody.

"Come in," he said sarcastically. "Don't mind the
way I'm dressed. This is Liberty Hall; you can spit on
the mat and call the cat a bastard."

Then he realized that she was in a very distressed
state, her face white, her mouth trembling. Her shirt
was ripped, exposing her right breast. She was holding
her shorts, the waistband of which had been ripped,
up with one hand.

"What happened, Susie?" he demanded.

She stared at him wildly then whispered, "Hodge
thought that I'd be safe here as long as nobody else
knows. . . ."

"But what happened?"

She tried to pull herself together. "A party, in the officers' mess. . . . That band of heroes. . . ." A spark of humor was showing through. "All for one and one for all. . . . The trouble was that I was supposed to be the one. . . ."

"But surely the general. . . ."

"His officers can do no wrong."

"Or Paul, and Lania. . . ."

"Lania's never forgiven me for having been Paul's lover. . . . And Paul? He's well under *her* thumb. . . ."

Then she screamed, tried to hide herself behind Grimes. He was acutely conscious of that bare breast pressing against the naked skin of his back. The door opened. It was Hodge again.

He grunted, "Grimes's tucker time, ain't it? Here's sandwiches an' a bottle o' plonk. Enough for both of you."

"And what about . . . *them?*" whispered Susie.

"They're happy enough now. They got those hen sergeants up. The last I saw of the party they certainly weren't missing *you*. But you're safer out of sight for a while." He leered, but somehow not offensively. He thrust the burdened tray into Grimes's hands, saying, "Candy is dandy but liquor is quicker."

He turned and left, shutting the door decisively behind him.

Grimes put the laden tray down on the desk. Susie sat down on the narrow bunk. She pulled a packet of cigarillos from the breast pocket of her shirt—the side that was not torn—put one of the slim, brown cylinders in her mouth with a hand that had almost stopped trembling, puffed it into ignition. She extended the pack to Grimes. "Smoke, Captain?"

"Thank you."

He lit up.

She regarded him through the eddying fumes. She managed a slight smile. She said, "If anybody had told me, while I was a stewardess in the Met. Service, that I'd feel safe locked up in a dogbox with a hairy-arsed space captain I'd have called him a bloody liar."

"Mphm." Grimes put an exploratory hand to his smooth buttocks. "I'm not hairy," he said.

"A figure of speech."

She got up from the bunk, brushed past Grimes to get to the desk. She unscrewed the plastic cap—large enough to be used as a cup—of the bottle, filled it. She said, "I have to admit that General Mortdale's senior mess sergeant can *do* things with an autochef. Here. Try it."

Grimes sipped cautiously. This was his first alcoholic drink for a very long time. It was a fortified wine, not too sweet, with a not unpleasant flavor and aroma that he could not identify. He sipped again, with less caution.

Susie took the cup from him, raised it to her own lips. "To a glorious restoration," she said. She drank. "And death and destruction to the enemies of our gracious prince and his princess." She drank again. "And may they always be successful in protecting the tender bodies of their loyal female subjects from their brutal and licentious soldiery!"

"They haven't had much success so far," said Grimes nastily.

"And don't I bloody well know it, John! (You don't mind, do you?)" She refilled the cup. "I'm neither a virgin nor a prude—but I do draw the line at pack rape. And I do think that Their High and Mightinesses should take a damn sight more interest in what their gallant soldiers get up to. This effort tonight wasn't the first time, you know. I've been fighting those bastards off ever since they came aboard on Porlock, knowing all the time that the only one to whom I could look to help was Hodge."

"Then why did you go to the party?"

"Lania—*Her Highness*—told me that as the catering officer of this noble vessel I must be there to see that the pongoes didn't starve or die of thirst. . . ."

"*You're* in no danger of doing the latter," said Grimes.

"Sorry, John." She took a swig from the refilled cup,

then handed it to him. "But as I was saying—I do draw the line at pack rape. And at being beaten up for foreplay. Look!" She stripped off her torn shirt, stepped out of her shirt, peeled down her minimal underwear. She pointed at a dark bruise on the pale skin of her upper right thigh, at another on her round belly, another one just below the prominent pink nipple of her left breast.

Suddenly Grimes felt a flood of sympathy. Until now he had not really believed the girl's story, had been asking himself how much of the girl's distress was genuine, how much mere play acting. But those bruises were real enough.

He said with feeling, "The bastards! I wish. . . ."

She laughed shakily. "You wish that you had the authority to throw them into the brig, or even out of the airlock without a spacesuit! I wish it too. But it makes me a little happier to think that the bloody general and his bloody colonels and majors got nowhere with me, whereas you. . . ."

The invitation was unmistakable. Grimes looked at her. Those bruises may have been ugly but they somehow accentuated the sexuality of her abundant nakedness. Her eyes were wide, staring at his own nudity. He felt himself responding. Her scarlet mouth, with its smeared lip pigment, was wide, inviting—but the thought of the mouths of the drunken soldiers crushed to hers almost put him off. He put the cup down on the desk, stooped to pick up her torn shirt, used it to wipe her face.

She laughed shakily, "Gods! You're a fastidious bastard, John! But I don't blame you. I like you for it. And I'm clean where it counts."

He dropped the ripped garment, pulled her to him. If he had not enjoyed an alcoholic drink for a long time it was even longer since he had enjoyed a woman. And then, unbidden, the memory of how his sexuality had initiated the chain of circumstances culminating in his present predicament rose to the surface of his mind.

If it had not been for that erotic dream and those obscene animals. . . . His erection began to die.

But he was determined to take what was being offered
to him. The woman in the dream, he reasoned, had been
darkly auburn, with deeply sun-bronzed skin. . . . The
actual woman in his arms was blonde, pale-skinned,
ample, not slender.

They kissed—and his first contact of sensitive mem-
branes drove the horrible memories back into the pit
from which they had risen. She was not only a woman
but a new woman, a new—to him—kind of woman.
There was a resilient softness such as he had never
experienced before; all of his past loves had tended
to be small breasted, slender limbed.

She fell backward onto the bunk, pulling him with
her. He was on her, in her. The coupling was fast—too
fast—explosive, mutually unsatisfying. She squirmed
from under him, got to her feet, smiled down at him.
She said, "You'll have to do better next time, John."
She refilled the wine cup, brought it to him. They shared
the liquor and a cigarillo, saying little. Then, stretched
beside him, gently and unhurriedly, her mouth and
hands skillful, she brought him to a fresh arousal.

The second time was better, much better. They made
love unhurriedly, experimentally, inventively, deferring
the climax again and again. At last they could hold out
no longer. Then, simultaneously (it seemed) they fell
into a deep, exhausted sleep.

They awoke. Grimes was hungry. The sandwiches
were inclined to be stale now but there was some wine
left to wash them down. After the meal, such as it was,
Susie went through to the bathroom. Grimes heard the
shower running and then, above the sound of descending
water, the noise of somebody making a fuss of opening
the padlock outside the door.

Hodge came in. He grinned at Grimes, said cheer-
fully, "*Their* party's over. They're sleeping it off. An'
how was *your* party, Grimes?"

Grimes said, "Thank you for the wine."

"Is that all you're thanking me for?" The engineer

was looking pointedly at the obviously fresh stains on the mattress cover. "Oh, Susie!"

"Yes?" came her voice from the bathroom.

"I brought you a fresh uniform from your cabin. The one that you were wearing when I saw you last looked a bit tattered. It's probably worse now." He put the bundle of clothing on the bunk then called, "I'll wait outside till you're dressed."

He left the cabin. Susie came out from the bathroom. She looked rather sluttish with her hair still wet from the shower—but, thought Grimes, none the worse for that.

She slowly put on the fresh shirt, saying, "Dear Hodge . . . I don't know what I'd have done without him. . . ." She noticed Grimes's jealous expression, laughed. "He's my half brother. Father played around a bit in his younger days."

"Mphm," grunted Grimes.

She stepped into her shorts. She was one of those women, thought Grimes, who looked better naked. Dressed, she was just another plump girl.

He went into the bathroom. The shorts and shirt that he had hung up to dry were damp again; Susie had not thought to shift them to where they would be safe from her splashings. But he put them on. They would dry out on his body soon enough.

When he reentered the cabin Susie was talking with Hodge. They turned to face Grimes. Susie said, "Are you with us, John?"

"What do you mean?" he asked.

"From now on we're looking after ourselves. We've decided that Paul and Lania have forfeited all claims to our loyalty."

"Why did you join up with them in the first place?" asked Grimes.

"We didn't know what they'd be like once they started to rise to what they think are their rightful positions. We didn't know what their supporters—if that mob from Porlock are any sample—were really like. But we know now.

"Oh, we'll play along for the time being. We have to. But we'll watch how the cards fall. If we see a chance to take a trick or two for ourselves we grab it.

"And you, John?"

He said, "If I were being paid I'd be only the hired help. But as I'm not being paid I'm not even that. All that I want is to get back to Bronsonia and my own ship."

"Stick with us," she told him, "and you might do just that."

Chapter 12

Grimes said, "I don't see how I can refuse to land on Dunlevin. But surely there will be some opposition. I can't imagine a convenient Aerospace Controllers' strike, such as there was on Porlock; on highly regimented, socialist planets you just don't strike if you know what's good for your health. . . ."

Susie and Hodge sat side by side on the settee, watching him as he ate his meal from the tray on the desk, listening to him as he talked between mouthfuls.

Grimes went on, "All that I know about Dunlevin is from those propaganda magazines that you brought me, Susie. They can hardly be classed as pilot books. They don't tell me what artificial satellites are in orbit about Dunlevin. There must be some. Are they armed? After the way in which the Duchy of Waldegren attempted to intervene in the civil war I should be very surprised if they aren't. Are they manned?"

He took and chewed another mouthful, swallowed.

"And talking of that—I've been meaning to ask for some time—just why does Bronsonia have manned meterological satellites while almost every other world makes do with fully automated stations in orbit?"

"The Jobs For Humans movement was very powerful on Bronsonia," said Hodge. "It still is, come to that. But there were some jobs that the humans didn't find all that attractive. That's why the met. stations are manned by almost unemployables . . ."

"Speak for yourself," snapped Susie.

". . . and misfits, such as ourselves and Their Sublime Highnesses."

"Mphm. But to return to Dunlevin. . . . Almost certainly orbital forts, probably manned. A continuous long-range radar watch. Mass Proximity Indicators? No. When you're sitting on, or in relatively close orbit about, something with the mass of a planet that mass is the only mass that registers. So, as long as we're making our approach under interstellar drive we're undetected—but once we break through into the normal continuum people are liable to start throwing bricks at us. . . ."

"Anybody would think," said Susie, "that you *want* to make a successful landing on Dunlevin."

"It's an interesting problem," admitted Grimes. "Too, as you've said, we have to play along—and to play along we have to stay alive. So I'll land this bloody ship for Paul and Lania. Presumably they, as soon as we're down, will be marching down the ramp at the head of their glorious army of liberation to be welcomed with open arms by the grateful peasantry. They hope. And *I* hope that they leave only a small guard detail on board. . . ."

"Coping with them should be no problem," said Susie.

It should not be, thought Grimes. Presumably the girl, with access to the ship's medicine chest, should be able to drug the soldiers' food or drink.

"There's still the problem of getting through the Dunlevin screen in one piece," said Hodge. "But suppose we do, and suppose that we're able to seize the ship—we've got it made. A navigator, an engineer and a catering officer. There's nowhere in the galaxy we can't go."

The door was flung open. One of Mortdale's aides—it was Major Briggs, Grimes realized—stood in the opening. He glared at Grimes and at Hodge, reserved an especially venomous look for Susie.

He snarled, "Fraternizing with the prisoner, are you? The general will hear of this."

Hodge made an ostentatious display of his pistol, said,

"Their Highnesses' orders have always been that the prisoner is to take his meals under guard."

"Guards," snapped Briggs, "should remain standing, not sprawl all over whatever seating is available."

"I'm a spaceman," growled Hodge. "Not a soldier."

"Do not belabor the obvious, Mr. Hodge. And now, Captain Grimes, if you've quite finished your Lucullan repast would you mind accompanying me to Control?" He made an imperative gesture with his pistol. "Up!"

Grimes wiped his mouth, deliberately slowly, with the paper napkin, then got to his feet. He preceded the major up the spiral staircase to the control room.

Lania, Paul and General Mortdale were awaiting him there, sitting at ease in the command chair and the two seats flanking it. Grimes, with Briggs at his side, stood before them. Nobody told him to sit; he decided that for him to do so would only cause unpleasantness.

Lania asked, "Have you given any thought to the problem of an unobserved landing on Dunlevin, Grimes? After all, you are—or were—a naval officer rather than a merchant spaceman. You must have made a study of strategy and tactics."

Mortdale interrupted. "As I have already said, Highness, space-borne invasions are the concern of the officers commanding the troops as well as of those commanding the transports. What do you know about the Gunderson Gambit, Captain Grimes?"

"Only what I have read, General. As a matter of fact I was thinking that it might be applied in this case. . . . If this were a warship—which she's not—I'd consider that attempting to take out the orbital forts would be less risky."

"This Gunderson Gambit . . ." asked Paul, "Is it risky?"

"Less risky, I think," said Grimes, "than trying to slip past the forts unobserved in normal space-time."

"It has been tried—the Gunderson Gambit, I mean?" asked Lania.

"By Commodore Gunderson, during the investment of Tallis. It worked for him."

"But it didn't work, General, for Captain Tanner during the first Waldegren campaign, or for Captain Lake at the Battle of Kahbil."

"It could work for Captain Grimes at the Battle of Bacon Bay," said Mortdale.

"Bacon Bay?" asked Grimes. The name reminded him of something, some historical military disaster.

"Yes, Captain. According to our Intelligence that will be the best place for a landing. The majority of the population is disaffected."

"But this Gunderson Gambit?" demanded Lania. "It's all very well for you military technicians to enjoy an entertaining—to yourselves—discussion but please remember that the ultimate decision rests with. . . ." The unspoken word "me" might just as well have been said aloud. She looked at her consort. "With His Highness," she finished.

Paul squirmed in his seat. Already, thought Grimes, the man was scared shitless.

"You explain, Captain," ordered Mortdale. "You're the spaceman."

"As you know, Highness," said Grimes to Lania, "the interstellar drive propagates a temporal precession field. Normally it is shut down before a close approach is made to a planetary body. . . ."

"The Van Allens?" murmured the woman. "I recall that when we got away from Bronsonia we did not proceed under Mannschenn Drive until we were clear of the Van Allen Belts."

"There is no actual risk involved, these days, in running the Van Allens with the drive in operation. It's not usually done because crew and passengers—passengers especially—can be scared by the brush discharges from every metal projection. Come to that, there is no actual danger, physical danger, that is, if you run right through a planet or even a sun; relative to a ship proceeding under Mannschenn Drive such bodies exist in an alternate universe. Of course, if the drive went on the blink at just the wrong place at the wrong time it would be just too bad for the ship and her people—and for the inhabitants of a populated world if a spaceship suddenly materialized somewhere under the surface. And as for suns—such an accident might trigger off a nova. There's only one way of finding out for sure and nobody's keen on trying it."

"Fascinating as these horror stories are," said Lania coldly, "I shall be obliged if you will come to the point."

"Very well, Highness. The Gunderson Gambit involves running in as close as you dare under Mannschenn Drive and then . . . materializing. If you've miscalculated very badly you break through into the normal continuum below the surface of the planet. The result is a Big Bang with the ship at Ground Zero. There's also a Big Bang if you materialize at anything below stratospheric level. But where can you say that a planet's atmosphere ends? If the sudden mixture of ship's matter and planetary matter occurs at an altitude where the planetary matter is no more than a few stray molecules and atoms of assorted gases you should suffer only a few casualties, with luck not even fatal ones. There should be no great damage to the ship's structure or to her machinery. The major risk will be a descent of at least six hundred kilometers with your inertial drive making enough racket to awaken even the sleepiest sentries."

"We didn't wake any sentries on Porlock," said Lania.

"On Porlock, Highness," said Mortdale, "nobody was on the alert for an armed invasion. Furthermore, the authorities were turning a blind eye and a deaf ear to our coming and going." He turned to Grimes. "But the people on the world on which your Commodore Gunderson was landing were, presumably, expecting trouble. What did *he* do?"

"He modified his ship while he was still outside the range of planet- and satellite-based radar, then made a powered, stern-first approach. He shut down his Mannschenn Drive at superstratospheric altitude, then fell free, using his inertial drive, initially, only to maintain attitude. Finally, only seconds before impact, he slammed on full vertical thrust *and* fired his auxiliary reaction drive. It worked—for the commodore. But this ship—a merchantman, not a warship—doesn't run to auxiliary rockets."

"But even without reaction drive," stated rather than asked Mortdale, "you can do it."

"The last part, General, yes. At least, I'll try. But the powered, stern-first approach is out.

"Why, Captain Grimes?"

"To begin with, it would mean that our entry into the atmosphere, even with the inertial drive shut down for the final free fall, would be at far too high a velocity. As I've already said, we don't have braking rockets to use before set-down. And we don't have the heat shields that a warship has. We'd hit the ground as a blob of molten metal.

"Our approach will have to be a normal one apart from our shutting down Mannschenn Drive within the Van Allens. We have to swing on the gyros, of course, so that we fall stern first to the target area. If anybody happens to be watching they'll see us appear suddenly on their radar screens—and they'll see, too, that we're just falling. There'll be panic stations—even if they assume that we're a meteorite and not a spaceship. At best—as far as we're concerned—there'll be an evacuation of the strike area. At worst there'll be an attempt to destroy the hunk cosmos debris—if they *are* fooled —before it strikes. And we don't run to antimissile laser or antimissile missiles."

The general grinned, quite amicably. "It is refreshing to discuss strategy and tactics with a man of your training, Captain. Most of my own officers are somewhat amateurish. But our main problem is one of a silent approach. We have our sympathizers, of course, on Dunlevin, a royalist underground. As soon as you can give me a firm ETA, a Carlottigram will be sent from this ship, allegedly emanating from a passenger aboard *Alpha Puppis,* to an elderly lady living in the capital city, Dunrobin. Innocent birthday greetings unless you have the key to the code. . . . We have people in the planet-based radar stations and also in the fortress satellites. There will be brief—very brief—breakdowns, failures to observe what is showing on the screens, at just the right—for us—time. . . ."

"Aren't they taking a great risk, those radar operators?" asked Grimes.

"They will be well rewarded," said Lania.

If they're lucky, thought Grimes. *If they're bloody lucky.*

"But can they be trusted?" asked Paul. "Can they be trusted?"

"You should never have gotten into this," Lania told him, "if you haven't the guts to see it through."

Grimes wondered how long Paul would last if the counterrevolution were successful but told himself, as he looked at the flabby prince, that he could hardly care less.

All that he wanted to do was to get down onto Dunleven in one piece and then, as soon as possible, to leave in the same intact state.

Chapter 13

As the voyage drew to its conclusion Grimes was required more and more frequently in Control. Few were the opportunities when he could discuss with Susie and Hodge their plan of campaign after a landing had been made—*if* a landing was made—and fewer still were the opportunities to have the girl to himself. Their sessions of lovemaking were brief, infrequent but torrid. He knew—and she knew—that what was between them could not last, not even if they survived the landing, not even if they succeeded in making their escape from Dunlevin. The transitory nature of their relationship made it all the more intense.

They had time to talk, sometimes, after their couplings. Once Grimes said to her, "You told me, some time ago, that Lania hates you because you were once Paul's lover. I just can't see how a girl like you could fall for a fat slob like him. . . ."

She laughed, a little ruefully. She said, "He wasn't always so fat. And back on Bronsonia—at least to the refugees and their children, such as myself—he was the Prince, the Prince Charming. Many native Bronsonians thought of him that way as well." She laughed again. "I believe you're jealous, John. . . ."

He laughed, but without real humor. "Perhaps I am."

And then Hodge, outside the cabin, made his usual major production of unlocking the door.

On another occasion they were talking of less personal matters.

He asked her, "What do you know of Bacon Bay, Susie?"

"About as much as you," she told him. "It's on the west coast of New Ireland. I suppose it was named after some personality among the original colonists. . . ."

He said, "There was a Bacon Bay—no, not Bacon Bay but a name very similar—back on Earth. I remember it from a history lesson years ago, when I was just a school kid. One of the American presidents made a landing there in support of a counterrevolution. . . ."

"And what happened?"

"It came unstuck."

She said, "I have a sort of presentiment that this one will. It's just as well, I think, that we won't be sticking around to find out just what does happen. . . ."

For a change Hodge was watching Grimes eat while Susie kept guard outside.

He said, "I've been helping the general's artificers with the hovertanks. Nasty, vicious little three-man jobs. . . . One driver, two gunners. . . . You're an expert on military matters, Grimes; perhaps you could tell me why Mortdale is going to use ground forces instead of a fleet of armed pinnaces? After all, we could have loaded quite a few aboard this ship. . . ."

"A lot depends," said Grimes, "upon what arms he was able to purchase on Porlock. Quite possibly the Porlockers didn't have any military aircraft to spare."

"Those tanks," said Hodge, "were manufactured in the Duchy of Waldegren."

"And so what? They could still be Porlockian surplus army equipment. But tanks instead of aircraft for the invasion? It makes sense. Aircraft—or spacecraft operating inside or outside an atmosphere—are fine for blowing the hell out of the enemy's military installations and/or centers of population—but they're also fine targets themselves. And if you want to take *and hold*, without causing overmuch damage, you need infantry. And tanks are sort of mechanized infantry."

"They can take and hold as much as they like," said Hodge, "as long as they don't hold *us*."

"This looks like being the last time, John," said Susie. "The last time, that is, on this leg of the voyage. I hope that it's not the last time, period."

"I do, too."

"That's up to us, the three of us," she said.

He looked suspiciously at her naked belly. It seemed a little plumper than usual.

She laughed. "By the three of us I meant you, Hodge and myself. Don't worry about any other possible meaning to my words. I'm taking my shots."

"Just as well," said Grimes. "I've enough worries already."

"*You* worried? I've heard that when you were in the Survey Service you were notorious for your good luck."

"If my luck had held," he said, "I shouldn't be here now."

"You bastard!" she said, and Grimes had to talk hard and fast before she would allow him to continue with the lovemaking.

When they were finished he said, "But, after all, I have been lucky. This time with you. . . ."

She said, "You don't deserve it."

Chapter 14

Bronson Star passed through Dunlevin's Van Allens, the natural screen of particles held about the planet by its magnetic field. The transit should have been made in nanoseconds of subjective time—but, with the Mannschenn Drive still in operation seemed to occupy an eternity. Grimes had read and had been told of the weird effects that might be expected, had warned the others—but reading about something in a book is altogether different from experiencing it in actuality.

There were the brush discharges from projections, crackling arcs between points. But a brush discharge should not look like a slowly burgeoning flower of multicolored flame; an arc, to a human observer in normal space-time, flares into instant existence, it is not a tendril of blinding incandescence slowly writhing from one terminal to the other. It crackles; it does not make a noise like a snake writhing with impossible slowness through dead leaves.

Grimes was surprised when his hand moved at quite normal speed. He stopped the Mannschenn Drive. The thin, high whine of the ever-precessing rotors deepened in tone to an almost inaudible hum, ceased. Ahead, as seen through the transparent dome of the control room, the writhing nebulosity that had been Dunlevin solidified to a great crescent, bright against the blackness of space. But Grimes's first concern was swinging the ship. He activated the directional gyroscopes, heard the initial rumble as they started, felt the tugs and pressures of centrifugal force.

He was aware that the transition to the normal continuum had not been without effects. There had been brief, intensely bright sparks in the air of the control room to tell of the forced matings of molecule with gaseous molecule. There was the acridity of ozone. An alarm buzzer was sounding. Grimes managed a hasty glance at the console, saw that the warning noise and the flashing red light signified the failure of nothing immediately important; for some reason one of the farm-deck pumps was malfunctioning. It would have to wait for attention.

Nothing—apart from a brief, burning pain in his right foot—seemed to be wrong with his own body. Had it been his heart, or his brain, the result could have been —would have been—disastrous. He watched the stern vision screen, saw the night hemisphere of Dunlevin swing into view.

The general—he, alone, had lived on the planet, had fought on the losing side in the civil war—gave Grimes his instructions. He said, "That major concentration of city lights is Dunrobin. The one to the right of it, the smaller one, is Dunrovin. . . . Below it, on your screen, is Dunsackin. . . ."

The piratical ancestors of the exiled royalty and aristocracy, thought Grimes, had displayed a rather juvenile sense of humor when they renamed the planet and its major cities. He knew, having studied the charts, that Dunrobin was now Freedonia, Dunrovin changed to Libertad and Dunsackin to Marxville. . . . A pile of shit by any name still stinks, he told himself sourly.

"Try to fall," ordered Mortdale, "midway between Dunrovin and Dunsackin. Before too long we shall pick up a laser beacon, like the one that you homed on when you landed on Porlock."

"If it is there," said Lania—for the benefit, thought Grimes, of the pale, trembling Paul. Then, just to show impartiality in her distribution of psychological discomfort, "You needn't be so fussy about avoiding the thing this time, Grimes. You can't make an omelet without breaking eggs—or a counterrevolution without breaking beacons."

Ha, thought Grimes. *Ha, bloody ha! And we'll soon see who has the last laugh!*

But he could no longer afford the luxury of indulging in sardonic thoughts. The ship was falling like a stone, a meteorite. Soon she would be leaving a trail in the night sky like one. As long as that was the only indication of her arrival she might be taken for a natural phenomenon but if the flaring descent were accompanied by the hammering of inertial drive it would be a dead giveaway. He must use the drive now while the vessel was still in a near vacuum, incapable of conducting sound.

He applied lateral thrust, brought the bull's eye of the stern vision screen exactly midway between the lights of the two cities, held it there. As on past occasions he was forgetting that he was a prisoner acting under duress, at gunpoint. He was beginning to enjoy himself. He had a job to do, one demanding all his skills.

Bronson Star fell.

Her skin was heating up but not—yet—dangerously so. She was maintaining her attitude—so far, but once she was in the denser atmospheric levels she would be liable to topple. In a properly manned ship Grimes would have had officers watching instruments such as the radar altimeter, the clinometer, external pressure gauge and all the rest of them while he concentrated on the actual pilotage. Now he was a one-man band. All that his companions in the control room were good for was pointing their pistols at him.

Bronson Star fell.

The air inside the ship was becoming uncomfortably warm and the viewports were increasingly obscured by upsweeping incandescence. But the stern vision screen was clear—and in it, quite suddenly, appeared a tiny, red-glowing spark, a little off-center.

Inertial drive again, lateral thrust, sustained, fighting inertia. . . . The ship responded sluggishly but she did respond, at last. Grimes was sweating but it was not only from psychological strain. It was no longer warm in the control room; it was hot and becoming hotter.

"You'll burn us all up!" screamed Paul.

"Be quiet, damn you!" snarled Lania.

Bronson Star fell.

The radar altimeter read-out on the stern vision screen was a flickering of numerals almost too rapid to follow. The beacon light was still only a spark but one of eye-searing intensity—or was the smarting of Grimes's eyes due only to the salt perspiration that was dripping into them?

Bronson Star started to topple.

Lateral thrust again. The ship groaned in every member as she slowly came back to the vertical relative to the planetary surface.

Grimes realized that somebody else had come into the control room.

"General!" shouted a voice—that of Major Briggs? "General! The men are roasting down there! They'll be in no state to fight even if they're still alive when we land!"

The troop decks, converted cargo holds, would not be as well insulated as was the accommodation, thought Grimes. They must be ovens. . . .

"General! You must stop before we're all incinerated!"

"Captain Grimes," ordered Mortdale at last, "you may put the brakes on."

Easier said than done, thought Grimes. But to slow down at this altitude would be safer than carrying out the original plan. He could apply vertical thrust gradually—but, even so, it must sound to those in the countryside below the ship as though all the hammers of hell were beating in the sky. And what of the planet's defenses? Were military technicians sitting tensely, their fingers poised over buttons?

Had they already pushed those buttons?

In the screen the figures presented by the radar altimeter were no longer an almost unreadable flicker. The rate of descent was slowing yet there was not—nor would there be for a long time—any appreciable drop in temperature. But the thermometer had ceased to rise and only an occasional veil of incandescent gases obscured the viewports.

Grimes increased vertical thrust. The ship complained, trembled. Loose fittings rattled loudly. Relative to the surface below her *Bronson Star* was now almost stationary.

"Drop her again!" ordered Mortdale.

That made sense. It might possibly fool a computer; it almost certainly would fool a human gunlayer.

The hammering of the inertial drive abruptly ceased. Again the ship fell—but there was no burgeoning flower or flame in the sky above her, where she had been.

A suspicion was growing in Grimes's mind. This landing—apart from the problems of ship handling—was all too easy. Intelligence works both ways, and there are double agents. But he said nothing. If the general knew his job—and what had he been in the old Royal Army? a second lieutenant?—he would be smelling a rat by now.

The altimeter was unwinding fast again and, in the screen, that solitary beacon was blindingly bright.

1,000 . . . 900 . . . 800 . . . 700 . . .

Vertical thrust again. No matter who else might want *Bronson Star* in one piece Grimes most certainly did.

600 . . . 550 . . .

Still too fast, thought Grimes.

500 . . . 450 . . .

He increased vertical thrust.

430 . . . 410 . . . 390 . . .

"Get us *down!*" snarled Lania. "Get us down, damn you!"

Free fall again, briefly. Then full vertical thrust. Again *Bronston Star* shook herself like a wet dog as the inertial drive hammered frenziedly.

10 . . . 5 . . . 3 . . . 1 . . .

It was not one of Grimes's better landings. The ship sat down hard and heavily with a bone-jarring jolt. Had the great vanes of her tripedal landing gear not been equal to the strain she would surely have toppled, become a wreck. The shock absorbers did not gently sigh; they *screamed*.

"Airlocks open!" ordered Mortdale. "Ramps out!" Then, to Paul, "You, Your Highness, will lead the invasion. A hovertank, in which you will ride, carries your personal standard."

"I should stay here, in headquarters," said Paul weakly.

"You must show your flag, Highness. And your face."

"It is just as well," said Lania, "that his flag doesn't match his face. We don't want to surrender before we've started."

"Somebody has to keep guard over Grimes to make sure that he doesn't try anything," persisted Paul.

"It won't be you," said Lania.

"Major Briggs has his orders," said the general.

Chapter 15

Grimes was hustled down to his quarters by Briggs and two sergeants, locked in. He sat glumly on the settee, smoking his pipe, trying to visualize what was happening. Sonic insulation muffled interior noises but he could faintly hear shouts, mechanical whinings and clankings. The little hovertanks would be streaming down the ramps, followed by the heavier tracked vehicles. He strained his ears for the sound of gunfire, of exploding missiles, heard nothing but the diminishing bustle of disembarkation. It seemed that the landing was unopposed.

Then there was silence save for the murmurings of the ship's own life processes. The air flowing in through the ventilation ducts was cooler now, bore alien scents, some identifiable, some not. The smell of the seashore predominated; a brininess, the tang of stranded seaweed. This was to be expected; *Bronson Star* had landed just above the high-water mark on the beach at Bacon Bay. Hodge was flushing out the ship's stale atmosphere with the fresh, sea air.

Grimes's sweat-soaked clothing dried on his body. He would have liked to have stripped, showered and laundered his garments but knew that he must maintain himself in a state of instant readiness. Were Susie and Hodge playing their parts? he wondered. Had the girl served drugged food and drink to Briggs and his sergeants? Had the engineer readied the ship for immediate lift-off?

The door opened and Susie stood there. As on a past

73

occasion her clothing was in disarray, her shirt torn, her ample breasts exposed.

She swore, "That bald-headed bastard Briggs! The sergeants went out like a light—but not him! Two mugs of coffee with enough dope to put a regiment to sleep and still he stayed on his feet! Hodge had to put a dent in his sconce with a wrench while he was trying to strangle me." She grinned viciously, "But whoever finds him where we left him—either Lania or the Free People's Army—will treat him much more roughly!"

Grimes brushed past her, ran up the spiral staircase to Control; it was faster than waiting for the elevator. Before sitting in the command seat he looked out through the viewports, towards the glow on the horizon that marked the city lights of Dunrovin—the royalist army's first objective. Then, between ship and city, an impossible sun suddenly rose, blinding despite the automatic polarization of the ports. Grimes ran to his chair, did not bother to strap himself in. He knew that he must get the ship up before the shock wave hit.

The inertial drive was already on Stand By. It commenced its metallic stammer at the first touch of Grimes's fingers on the controls. He did not—as he should have done, as in normal circumstances he would have done—nurse the innies up gradually to maximum thrust; he demanded full power at once and miraculously got it.

Nonetheless the initial lift-off was painfully slow.

Bronson Star groaned, shuddered. She climbed into the night sky like a grossly fat old woman reluctantly clambering upstairs to bed, wheezing and palpitating. Then the shock wave hit her, slamming her sidewise— but also upward. Grimes struggled with his controls, maintaining attitude. When the ship was once again upright he saw that she was making better speed, was climbing fast and faster.

Only then was Grimes able to check that all was ready—or had been ready—for lift-off. The airlock doors were all sealed, he saw; that was the most important thing. Life-support systems were functioning.

Susie—he had quite forgotten that she was in the control room with him—called out. "John! The radar! Somebody's after us!"

He heaved himself out of his chair, went to the screen tank of the all-around radar. Yes, there were intruders, six tiny sparks, astern but closing. He had no quarrel with them but it was reasonable to assume that they had a quarrel with him.

Perhaps—perhaps!—he would be able to talk his way to freedom.

He went to the NST transceiver, switched on. At once a strange voice came from the speaker, "Free People's Air Force to unidentified spacecraft. . . ." Obviously whoever was talking had been doing so for some time. "Free People's Air Force to unidentified spacecraft. . . . Free People's. . . . ."

"Bronson Star here," said Grimes.

"Land at once, *Bronson Star.* Resistance is useless. Your army and your leaders have been destroyed. Land at once, or we open fire."

And why all the talking? wondered Grimes. Why had not the spaceship been fired upon already? Why should people quite willing to wipe out an army with a nuclear landmine be reluctant to destroy a spaceship? Of course, he reasoned, *Bronson Star* would be a most welcome addition to the Dunlevin merchant service, but. . . Surely if *they* couldn't have her they would see to it that nobody else did.

He looked at the stern vision screen—and laughed.

The shock waves had not only given the ship a welcome boost; it had pushed her into a position directly above one of the cities. Which one he neither knew nor cared. He wondered if its people knew that they were, in effect, his hostages.

He told Susie, "Take over the NST. Keep 'em talking. I have to make sure that we stayed relatively put. . . ."

Back in his command chair he used lateral thrust to keep the city lights coincident with the bull's eye of the screen. He watched the altimeter figures steadily climbing. He heard Susie saying into the microphone,

"We are neutrals." We were skyjacked by Prince Paul and General Mondale. We were forced, at gunpoint, to bring them and their soldiers here. . . ."

"You must return for questioning. No harm will come to you if you are innocent. . . ."

"You have no jurisdiction over a Bronsonian space-ship. . . ."

"When she is in our airspace we have. Return to the surface at once."

"Ask them," said Grimes, " '*Straight down*?' "

Susie did so. She laughed. Grimes laughed—then remembered that he still had to get past the orbital forts. No matter what his position would be relative to Dunlevin's surface a cloud of radioactive dust and gases above the stratosphere would be little worry to anybody at ground level.

Chapter 16

He had hoped that the royalist invaders would create enough of a diversion to distract attention from *Bronson Star's* getaway. He had strongly suspected that the landing would not be a great surprise to the rulers of Dunlevin; he had not anticipated that the invading force, in its entirety, would be wiped out by nuclear blast. (Surely there could have been no survivors.) He had envisaged a nasty little battle but with fatal casualties deliberately kept to a minimum so that there could be a show trial afterward with public humiliation of Paul, Lania and their adherents. But military and political leaders do not always see eye to eye—and the military have always been prone to use steam hammers to squash gnats.

Meanwhile—how trigger happy were the crews of the fortress satellites? Would they shoot first and ask questions afterward or would they try to talk *Bronson Star* into surrender? (Their Air Force colleagues had given up the chase saying, before they turned away, "You've had your chance. You'll never get past the forts.") Did the satellite crews know about the Gunderson Gambit? It was supposed to be a closely guarded secret of the Federation Survey Service—but Mortdale knew (had known) about it. And if Mortdale had known. . . .

"Susie," he asked urgently, "was the general ever in the Marines? The Federation Survey Service Marines, that is. . . ."

"Why do you ask, John? He's dead now. What does it matter what he was."

Cold-blooded little bitch! thought Grimes angrily.

The general, with all his faults, had been more of Grimes's breed of cat than Paul and Lania or, come to that, Susie and Hodge.

"This is important," he said. "Was he ever in the Marines?"

"Yes," she admitted sulkily. "Quite a few of the refugees, the military types, entered Federation service. He got as high as colonel, I believe. . . ."

And as a colonel, thought Grimes, he'd have had had access to all manner of classified information. He hoped that there were no ex-colonels of Marines in the satellites. It was extremely unlikely that there would be.

He said, "Put the radar on long range. See if you can pick up any of the orbital forts."

She said, "There're all sorts of bloody blips—some opening, some closing. They could be *anything*."

"They probably are," said Grimes.

Then again a strange voice came from the transceiver. "*Fortress Castro* to *Bronson Star*. This is your last chance. Inject yourself into closed orbit and prepare to receive our boarding party—or we open fire!"

"You can't!" cried Susie to Grimes.

"I have to," he said. "Look at the gauges. You wouldn't be able to breathe what's outside the ship but it's still more atmosphere than vacuum. I can't risk the Gunderson Gambit—yet."

He had anticipated this very situation, reasoned that a show of compliance would be the only way to avoid instant destruction. Already he had thrown the problem into the lap of the computer; all that he had to do now was switch over from manual to automatic control.

"Inject into orbit!" came the voice of *Fortress Castro*. "We are tracking you. Inject into orbit—or. . . ."

"Tell them that we're injecting," said Grimes to Susie.

He threw the switch, heard and felt the arhythmic hammering of the drive as *Bronson Star* was pushed away from her outward and upward trajectory. He hoped that *Fortress Castro's* commander was relying more upon the evidence presented by his computer than the display in his radar tank. It would be some time before the ship's alteration of course would be visually obvious.

He got up from the command chair, went to his own radar. That large blip must be the orbital fort, that tiny spark moving away from it, toward the center of the screen, the vehicle carrying the boarding party. He turned his attention from the tank to the board with the array of telltale gauges; the dial at which he looked registered particle contact rather than actual pressure. Outside the ship there was vacuum to all practical intents and purposes—the practical intents and purposes of air-breathing organisms. But the sudden—it would have to be sudden—propagation of a temporal precession field would mean the catastrophic, intimate intermingling of those sparsely scattered atoms and molecules, those charged particles, with all matter, living and inanimate, within the ship.

At this distance from the planet the risk was still too great.

Grimes stared into the radar tank. Would *Bronson Star* reach apogee before the shuttle caught her? Would he be justified in using thrust to drive the ship to a higher altitude in a shorter time? He decided against this. *Fortress Castro's* computer would at once notify the shuttle's commander—and that vehicle was close enough now to use its light weaponry, automatic guns firing armor-piercing bullets that would pierce the shell of the unarmored *Bronson Star* with contemptuous ease, crippling her but not destroying.

"What the hell's going on up there?" came Hodge's voice from the intercom.

"We are temporarily in orbit," said Grimes. "I shall initiate Mannschenn Drive as soon as possible."

"I hope," said Susie—who, as a spaceperson of sorts, was beginning to get some grasp of the situation—"that it will be soon enough."

"Shuttle to *Bronson Star*," came a fresh voice from the NST transceiver. "Have your after airlock ready to receive boarders."

"Willco," said Susie, looking at Grimes, her eyebrows raised in unspoken query.

He grinned at her with a confidence that he did not feel.

The ship's computer, pre-programmed, took over. Grimes had forgotten to instruct it to sound any sort of warning before starting the Mannschenn Drive. He heard the hum of the rotors as they commenced to spin, the faint murmur that rapidly rose to a high-pitched whine. He saw colors sag down the spectrum, the warped perspective. And it was as though the control room had been invaded by a swarm of tiny, luminous bees, each miniscule but intense flare the funeral pyre of a cancelled-out atom. But there was no damage done—not to Susie, not to himself, not to the ship. And not, he hoped, to Hodge.

The pyrotechnic display abruptly ceased.

Grimes pulled his vile pipe out of his pocket, filled and lit it, looked up and out of the familiar—comforting now rather than frightening—blackness with the writhing, iridescent nebulosities that, in normal space-time, were the stars.

He said, "As soon as the mass proximity indicator shows that there's nothing dangerously close we'll set trajectory. And then . . . Bronsonia, here we come!"

"Not so fast," said Susie, her voice oddly cold. "Not so fast. *You* have only a few fines to pay on Bronsonia. Hodge and I face life imprisonment or rehabilitation. And that—need I tell you?—is just another word for personality wiping."

Chapter 17

Bronson Star broke away from Dunlevin without further incident. She was bound, at first, for nowhere in particular. Her inertial drive was running only to provide a comfortable half-standard gravity, her Mannschenn Drive was in operation only to make it virtually impossible for any Dunlevin warships—the Free People's Navy did, Grimes knew, possess two obsolescent frigates—to intercept her.

Grimes, Hodge and Susie sat around the table in the wardroom. There was coffee—not very good. There was a bottle of some unnamed liqueur that had been distilled by the late General Mortdale's senior mess sergeant. Grimes, sipping the smooth, potent and palatable fluid, rather hoped that the noncommissioned officer had survived the Bacon Bay debacle; as he had been one of the two men left with Major Briggs to keep guard on the ship this was possible. The drugged soldiers had been dumped from the airlock, onto the beach, shortly prior to lift-off.

Grimes raised his glass in a toast. "Here's to Sergeant Whoever-He-Is. Here's to his continuing good health."

Susie said, a little sourly, "He was a good cook and even better at persuading the autochef to produce liquor. But I can't help feeling a bit sorry that we didn't kill the pongoes before we threw them out."

"Too many people died," said Grimes. "I rather hope that Briggs and the two sergeants didn't."

"And if they didn't," said Susie, "and if they were taken prisoner, they'll sing. They'll sing like a male voice trio—or, if the Free People's Secret Police is as bad as the Royalist Underground makes out, like a soprano trio."

"So," asked Grimes, "what?" He lifted and lit his pipe then continued. "Nobody on Dunlevin thinks that *Bronson Star* lifted off all by her little self. They know that she must have had a crew."

"And now," said Susie, "they know who was in the crew. The Underground will know—and what the Underground knows the royalist refugee enclaves on Bronsonia, Porlock and a few other planets will soon know."

"With your share of the salvage money you should be able to buy protection," said Grimes. "That's why I think we should return to Bronsonia as soon as possible. We—the three of us—won this ship back from Paul and Lania and their mob. Even though I was, at the time of the original seizure, employed by *Bronson Star's* owners, I was, legally, neither master nor crew member. My name was on neither the Articles nor the Register. The salvage claim should stick."

"And you want your share," said Susie, "to pay your fines and port dues so that you can get your own little ship back."

"Of course," agreed Grimes.

"I see your point, John. But you're not a known criminal. Hodge and I are. There was the first sky-jacking, remember. The met. satellite. Captain Walvis will not have forgotten how I massaged the back of his neck with a pistol muzzle while he broke out of orbit to intercept *Bronson Star*."

"You could claim," said Grimes, "that you acted under duress."

"Ha! And even if the court believed it, there'd still be the Dunlevin royalists out for revenge."

"We could go out to the Rim," contributed Hodge. "Change the ship's name, our own names. Set up shop as a one-ship tramp company."

"You've been reading too many space stories, Hodge," said Grimes. "That's the sort of thing that people do in fiction, never in fact. Known space is festooned with red tape. All—and I mean *all*—data concerning every merchant ship is fed into the memory banks of the Master Registry back on Earth—and those banks are instantly accessible to every port authority on every planet—on every planet that runs to a spaceport, that is. And those that don't haven't been discovered or settled yet."

"Surely we could *buy* false ship's papers and personal papers," said Hodge.

"Who from?" asked Grimes. "And, more importantly, what with?"

Susie laughed. "Mortdale brought the royalist war chest aboard at Porlock. Folding money, in good Federation credit bills. The accumulation of contributions from refugees such as my revered parents. . . . I haven't made a proper count yet—but there's plenty. Even if we can't—as you say—have the ship's identity changed we can pay to have ourselves . . . transmogrified? Is that the right word? But you know what I mean."

"But where?" said Grimes, more to himself than to the others. "But where? It can't be too far away; I want to get *Bronson Star* back to where she came from before there's too much of a hue and cry. Probably already the Survey Service has been ordered to keep its eyes skinned for us—and if they find us where we shouldn't be they'll be claiming the salvage money."

"Looking after yourself, Grimes," commented Hodge rather nastily.

Susie sprang to his defense. "And why shouldn't he? Nobody else is."

"*I* looked after him," grumbled the engineer. "If it hadn't been for me he'd never have gotten off Dunlevin."

"If it hadn't been for him," said Susie, "we'd never have gotten off Dunlevin. We'd be undergoing interrogation by the Secret Police right now."

"We're all in this," said Grimes. "But our ways have to part." He looked at Susie regretfully, and she at him in the same way. "I must get you to some world where you can use your ill-gotten gains to buy yourselves new lives. Then I must get myself back to Bronsonia to look after my own affairs."

"Without an engineer?" asked Hodge.

"I've covered quite a few light years in *Little Sister* without one. Of course, her engines are designed so as to require minimal maintenance. But the ones in this ship should hold out for the voyage from. . . . From? From wherever it is to Bronsonia. And if they don't . . . I'll just have to yell for help on the Carlotti—if that hasn't broken down, too."

"You could just drop us off somewhere in one of the boats," said Susie but looked relieved when Grimes refused to consider this expedient.

"We'll sleep on it," he said at last after several minutes more of fruitless discussion. He raised no objection when Susie accompanied him to the captain's quarters which, with the feeling that he was once more putting himself in his rightful place, he had reclaimed.

Chapter 18

Grimes got to sleep at last. (Susie had been demanding.)

He slept, cradled against her warm, ample resilience —and he dreamed. The noise of *Bronson Star's* engines —the subdued, arhythmic beat of the inertial drive, the thin, high whine of the ever-precessing Mannschenn rotors—wove itself into his dream. (Most dreams are based on memories and he had spent so much of his life aboard ships.)

He was back on board his first command, the little Survey Service courier *Adder*. He was entertaining a guest in his cabin, the humanoid but nonhuman envoy from Joognaan. Joognaan was not an important world, either commercially or strategically; had it been, the envoy would have traveled in far greater style than he was doing now, aboard a ship that had been referred to slightingly, more than once, as an interstellar mail van.

Balaarsulimaam—that was the envoy's name—had made his way to Earth in a variety of carriers. First there had been the star tramp that had dropped down to Joognaan for a small shipment of artifacts and a few casks of *talaagra*—a somewhat bitter wine that was prized, although not excessively so, by gourmets on one or two planets. His voyage—from world to world, in ship after ship—had been a sort of three-dimensional zigzag. On Earth he had seen the Minister for Galactic Trade but had been unable to interest that gentleman in his wares. The Federation government had not—by its own lights—been ungenerous, however. It had given Balaarsulimaam passage to Lindisfarne in the Survey

Service transport *Jules Verne* and from Lindisfarne on in the courier *Adder*, Lieutenant John Grimes commanding.

He had been a lonely little being, this Balaarsulima-am. In spite of indoctrination Survey Service officers did not like having aliens aboard their ships. In *Adder* there was a further complication—with the exception of Grimes none of the courier's people liked cats. The Joognaanards are cat-like—or kangaroo-like. Just as the mythical Centaur was half man and half horse, so the inhabitants of Joognaan are half cat and half kangaroo. They have only four limbs, however.

Grimes was less xenophobic than most and was something of a cat lover. He made Balaarsulimaan welcome in his quarters. He enjoyed talking with him over drinks and felt no repugnance when his guest lapped rather than sipped from his glass.

It was one such social occasion that he was reliving now in his dream.

He was saying, "I'm rather surprised, Balaarsulima-am, that you couldn't interest any of the importers back on Earth in your wine. After all—the major restaurants pride themselves on being able to serve foods and drinks from every world known to man. . . ."

The Joognaanard's pink tongue dipped into the wide-rimmed drinking vessel that Grimes had provided for him, worked busily. He slurped, then sighed.

"Captain," he said, "the business with our wine is like the business of Scottish whisky. What I am drinking now—and I thank you for your hospitality—does not come from Scotland. It comes from Rob Roy, a planet of the Empire of Waverley. I have enjoyed the real Scottish whisky on Earth. I am enjoying this. I am not a Scottishman and I cannot tell the difference. Can you?"

"I am not a Scotsman," said Grimes. "I can't."

"And Rob Roy is much closer to your Lindisfarne than is Scotland. The freight, therefore, is much less. The whisky, therefore, is much less costly. So it is with our *talaagra*. There is a wine that they make on Austral, which is close to Earth. Even I can hardly detect the difference between it and our wine. And it must come only a short way and so is charged little freight."

"I see," said Grimes.

"But it was not only wine that I was trying to sell. It was a service—a service that people would have to come to Joognaan to avail themselves of. Our doctors—I have learned from captains of starships who have come in with injured crew members—are very clever. They have the—how do you say?—the technical—no, technique to regrow, in a short time, injured members that have had to be removed."

"So do ours," said Grimes. "But regrowing is a long process. Most people prefer to shop around for replacements in a body bank."

"There was a young lady . . ." went on Balaarsulimaam. "She was, I think, a purser in one of the ships. Unwisely she had not gone to her cabin when the ship was landing. She was concerned about the safety of certain heavy cases in one of the storeplaces. A case fell on her, crushing her face and the upper part of her body. We remade her."

"But that could have been done on Earth," said Grimes. "On almost any of our worlds."

"But we—our doctors—remodeled her. Aboard the ship was a representation of some female entertainer, a thin woman. The girl had been fat, like Susie. . . ."

(With that last sentence Grimes, even in his sleep, realized that fantasy was mingling with actual memory.)

"We remade her so that she looked almost the twin of the entertainer."

"Body sculpture is practiced on most worlds," said Grimes.

"But it is a long process and very expensive. With our doctors it is not long, and it is not expensive. All that I asked your government was that a proper spaceport be constructed on Joognaan and that we be allowed to advertise on Earth and other planets. We have credits, from the sale of our pottery and our wine —enough for the advertising but not enough for a spaceport. I think that, at first, your Minister showed sympathy—but his advisers, the representatives of the Terran doctors, did persuade him that our way was not safe. It was all, somebody said to me in confidence, a matter of invested interests."

Grimes refrained from correcting the alien. His meaning was clear enough. Members of any profession are jealous of their mystiques.

"But I will show to you, Captain, what can be done. . . ."

Balaarsulimaam waved his three-fingered hand. The door to the day cabin opened. A woman stood there. She was quite naked. Her slender body was familiar, as it should have been, even to the mole over the small, firm left breast. But, incongruous above Maggie Lazenby's slim, smooth shoulders was the plump face of Susie.

Grimes woke up with a start.

He slid out of the wide bunk without waking the girl and made his way to Control, ordered the computer to start doing its sums.

A call at Joognaan wouldn't be too great a detour.

Chapter 19

"It's a good solution to your problems," said Grimes with as much conviction as he could muster. "Bala-arsulimaam will help. He assured me, before he left *Adder,* that he would be at my service if ever I returned to his world."

"Shipboard friendships," said Susie, "are woven from even flimsier threads than shipboard love affairs."

Grimes didn't like the way that she was looking at him as she said this and didn't like the way that Hodge chuckled.

He went on, "In any case, you can pay. . . ."

"As long as it's not too much," said Hodge grudgingly. "But just what do you have in mind?"

"A complete change of physical characteristics for Susie and yourself—even, to be on the safe side, to fingerprints and retinal patterns. One beauty of the Joognaan technique is that it doesn't take anything like as long as the body sculpture on human planets—so I'll stay around until I'm sure that the two of you will be all right, hoping that no odd star tramp blows in to find *Bronson Star* sitting there. An All Ships broadcast must have gone out, asking everybody to keep their eyes skinned for us, as soon as we vanished from Bronsonia.

"When I'm happy—and when you're happy, of course—I lift off, leaving you on Joognaan. You stay there—you'll have no option—until the next tramp drops in. Then you buy passage in her to wherever she's going next. Your story will be that you're clones, that the Joognaanards, after they'd performed regenerative surgery on one or two spacepersons, retained cell cultures for their own experimental purposes. Balaarsuli-maam will fix you up with the necessary papers."

"Nobody likes clones," stated Hodge dogmatically.

"Not when they know that they're clones," said Grimes. "Come to that, clones with money are no more unpopular than anybody else."

"A complete making over. . . ." said Susie thoughtfully. "Tell me, John, is the process painful?"

"I've been told that it's not."

She kneaded the flesh of her right thigh, below the hem of her shorts, with pudgy fingers. "Of course, it could be worth a little discomfort. I am just a bit overweight. . . ."

"I like you the way that you are," said Grimes gallantly—then wondered why he should remember that slim woman in his dream.

"And Hodge," she went on, "is no Adonis. . . ."

"I like me the way that I am," growled the engineer. "But I'm willing to sacrifice my beauty in return for safety."

"So it's decided, agreed upon," said Grimes.

"I don't altogether like it," muttered Susie. "And you haven't told us about your end of it. What story will you have to account for the long time it took you between Dunlevin and Bronsonia? How will you account for your being alone in *Bronson Star*? Everybody in Dunlevin will know by now that you weren't alone when you lifted off. Apart from anything else *I* handled the conversations with the Air Force and with the orbital fort."

"My story will be," said Grimes, "that the pair of you decided to take your chances in one of the ship's boats—and one of the boats will, of course, be missing from its bay by the time that I make planetfall at Bronsonia. After your escape the Mannschenn Drive broke down. It took me—all by myself, with no engineer to do the work—a long time to fix it. . . ."

"*You* couldn't fix a Mannschenn Drive," said Hodge.

"I have done so," Grimes told him. "Once. In *Little Sister*. I admit that she has only a glorified mini-Mannschenn, but even so. . . . Anyhow, I'd like you to fill me in on what sort of breakdown could be fixed by one man, not overly skilled."

"All right," said Hodge. "Your Mannschenn Drive breaks down. You bust a gut repairing it. Why, as a typical, bone-idle, spaceman branch officer don't you yell for help on the Carlotti?"

"Because," said Grimes, "I'm a money-hungry bastard. I don't want to have to split—or even lose entirely —the salvage money."

"And what about the auto-log?" asked Hodge. "That will carry a complete record of all use of main and auxiliary engines from Bronsonia on. It will show one set-down and lift-off too many."

"It won't," said Grimes, "after you've wiped it for me. A short circuit or whatever. I leave the sordid, technical details to you."

"You're a cunning bugger, Grimes," said Hodge with reluctant admiration.

"I try to be," said Grimes smugly.

Chapter 20

At that time there was no spaceport on Joognaan;
nor was there Aerospace Control. Some ships—those
that maintained the pretense of a service, albeit an extremely irregular one—announced their arrival with a
display of pyrotechnics, even if such fireworks were
only sounding rockets fired from superstratospheric
levels to the surface to give some indication of wind
directions and velocities. But there would be warning
enough for the natives as soon as *Bronson Star* was
well within the atmosphere; the clangor of her inertial
drive would give ample notice of her coming.

Grimes was obliged to rely heavily on his memories
of his one previous visit to the planet; there was very
little data concerning Joognaan in *Bronson Star's* memory banks. But he was sure that he would be able to
manage after making a rough visual survey from orbit.
All that he had to identify was the one city of any size
situated on a coastal plain, on the southern shore of a
wide estuary and with a high mountain range to the
eastward. The usual landing place for visiting starships
was to the south of the city in a wide clearing, an obviously artificial field set in a forest. From this a broad
road ran to the big town.

The old ship dropped through the morning air,
through the sparse scattering of high-altitude clouds
that had not been thick enough to obscure her objective. Susie sat with Grimes in the control room. There
was little that she could do to help as it was not necessary to man the NST radio. She spent most of the time

staring out through the wide viewports, exclaiming now and again as something caught her attention.

"Those must be ships down there. . . . The sort of ships that sail on the sea, I mean. . . . And there's a railway. . . ."

"Early industrial culture," said Grimes. "They're still a long way behind us in engineering. . . . But not in the medical sciences."

The clearing in the dark forest was showing up well in the stern vision screen. Grimes stepped up the magnification. There were no other spaceships in, which was all to the good. He reduced the scale again so that he could see something of the white road between city and clearing. There were a few moving black dots on it. So somebody was coming out to meet the ship. There would certainly be at least one linguist in the party, possibly Balaarsulimaam himself.

He concentrated on his pilotage, keeping the black circle that had been painted at the center of the landing field coincident with the bull's eye of the stern vision screen. He was having to make frequent applications of lateral thrust and the ship lurched as she fell through clear air turbulence. But at least, he thought, this time he wasn't bringing *Bronson Star* in with the evil, black eyes of at least three pistol muzzles looking at him.

He watched the presentation of radar altimeter readings, gradually slowed the rate of descent. At the finish the big ship was almost hovering, drifting down like a feather. Her vanes kissed the apron with the slightest of tremors rather than a jar.

She was down.

"We're here," said Grimes unnecessarily. He rang off the engines. He released himself from the command chair, went to the auxiliary control board and opened both inner and outer doors of the after airlock, extruded the ramp. He set the fans to work to flush out the ship with the fresh, forest air of Joognaan.

"Tell Hodge to join me at the airlock," he told Susie. "And you come along too."

He looked out from a viewport at the white road

that ran between the somber trees like a parting in dark hair. The steam-driven cars of the Joognaanards did not have far to come. There would have been time for him, however, to change into a decent uniform if he had had a decent uniform to change into—but most of his possessions were still aboard *Little Sister,* back on Bronsonia. The hapless Paul had left finery in the captain's cabin wardrobe but Grimes would sooner have gone naked than worn it.

He stood at the foot of the ramp with Hodge and Susie a little behind him. He looked along the wide avenue as the three vehicles, puffing loudly and pouring smoke and steam from their tall funnels, approached. Shafts of morning sun smote through gaps in the trees and were reflected from bright, polished brasswork, shone on glossy scarlet and emerald paintwork. One of them blew its whistle in greeting, a loud, cheerful tootle.

The high-wheeled, canopied, gaily painted cars trundled onto the apron. They stopped. Their passengers clambered out, six of them altogether. They hopped rather than walked toward the visitors. Were it not for their rather flat faces they would have looked like black-and-white furred, bushy-tailed kangaroos.

They came to a halt before the three humans, stood staring at them. The humans looked at the natives. Which of them was Balaarsulimaam? Grimes wondered. All the Joognaanards looked the same to him. Was Balaarsulimaam one of the party? Unless things had changed he must be; during those drinking and talking sessions aboard *Adder* Balaarsulimaam had divulged that he always greeted visiting space captains, had expressed doubts that his deputy, nowhere near as accomplished a linguist, would be able to cope during his absence.

One of the natives spoke. "Greetings, Captain Grimes. Have you come to have your ears diminished after all? The offer of our services still holds good."

Yes, remembered Grimes, Balaarsulimaam had made

that offer. He remembered, too, that there was a patch of black fur, an almost perfect six-pointed star, on the envoy's forehead. None of those with him were similarly marked; there were black patches aplenty but all of them irregular.

"Greetings, Balaarsulimaam," he said.

"Or have you come for trade, Captain Grimes? I see that it is a merchant vessel that you now command. I fear that we have little wine in our warehouses; the ship *Star Romany* was here only six rotations since. We have artifacts, should you desire them."

"You have already reminded me that you once offered your services."

"To give them will be our pleasure. When we have finished your ears will be as the tender petals of the *wurlilaya.*"

"Thank you," said Grimes. "But it is not my ears that I wish fixed. It is this young lady, and her companion."

"But they are not injured."

"Do you recall telling me about that purser who was badly injured? How, at her request, you remade her in the image of a female entertainer? That is what I want done—to the lady. And the man I also want changed."

Balaarsulimaam made the transition from old friend and shipmate to businessbeing. "How will you pay, Captain Grimes, for operations of such magnitude? What goods have you to barter? Were it merely a matter of your ears there would be no charge—but for this other I fear that there must be."

"We have no goods for barter," said Grimes, "but I remember that you told me that your people will now accept money in lieu. We can pay in Federation credits."

"That is good. We endeavor to save an amount sufficient for the purchase of a Carlotti transmitting and receiving station. May we come aboard to discuss terms?" Then, in what was obviously an attempt at humor, "I hope that you have remembered my taste in potable spirits."

"I remember," Grimes told him, "but I'm afraid that we have no whisky, Scotch or otherwise. But what we do have in the way of spirits is quite drinkable."

He led the way up the ramp.

Chapter 21

Balaarsulimaam was the only one of the party with any real command of standard English; the others just squatted on their haunches around the wardroom, lapping the brandy that was a fast-diminishing monument to Mortdale's mess sergeant, noisily nibbling sweet biscuits, conversing now and again among themselves in voices that reminded Grimes of a convocation of Siamese cats.

Balaarsulimaam himself did not talk much at first; he was interested in the brief and edited account of Grimes's adventures since they had last seen each other. He was told of the Bacon Bay fiasco; the version given him was something of a whitewash job on Susie and Hodge. According to it they had acted under duress as much as Grimes himself had done and were anxious to escape only from the vengeance of the royalist underground rather than from the processes of Bronsonian law.

Balaarsulimaam listened with apparent sympathy, although it was impossible for a Terran to discern any expression on that black-and-white furred face. Then he said that it would be possible for the biotechnicians to operate on Hodge and Susie and that their board and lodging until the next ship dropped in—probably in about thirty days—would present no problems. He promised to do his best to maintain the clone fiction should the visiting tramp master ask too many questions—although it had to be explained to him what a clone was.

It was then that Grimes began to have serious doubts

about Joognaan biological expertise—after all, the level
of technology on the planet was not high; at this moment of time the proud apex of mechanical evolution
was still the steam engine. And yet he had believed,
when he had been told it, the story of the injured purser
of the star tramp who had not only been healed but remodeled to her own specifications.

Balaarsulimaam named the price.

It was high—but nowhere nearly as high as a body-
sculpture job on Earth would have been.

Grimes looked at Susie; she knew to the last Federation Credit how much folding money had been
brought aboard at Porlock by General Mortdale. Susie
looked back at Grimes. She nodded.

"All right," said Grimes.

"You will be pleased by what we shall do," said
Balaarsulimaam.

"I hope so. I bloody well hope so, for that money,"
growled Hodge.

Susie glared at him.

"Then, tomorrow in the morning, I will call for you.
You, Miss Susie, and you, Mr. Hodge, will bring with
you representations of what you wish that your new ap-
pearances will be. Flat pictures will do, although if you
have—what do you call them?"

"Solidographs," supplied Grimes.

"Yes. They will be better."

"Where would *I* get a solidograph from?" demanded
Hodge.

"I'll find something for you," said Susie.

After the Joognaanards had left, Grimes and Susie
went for a stroll in the forest. This was definitely an
Earth-type—a very Earth-type apart from the dominant
species—planet, a fine example of parallel evolution.
To Grimes—who was no botanist—the trees were just
trees, the bushes just bushes, the flowers just flowers.
There were flying insects—great, gaudy butterflies,
other things like tiny, arthropodal bats. An animal that
scurried rapidly up a tree at their approach could have

been a Terran squirrel, had it not been for its long, rabbit-like ears.

They came to a pool in a clearing; the water looked very inviting. Grimes remembered that Balaarsulimaam had told him that Joognaan possessed no dangerous carnivores, no predators that would attack animals larger than themselves—and the indigenous humanoids were the biggest life form. Did that sweeping statement apply to aquatic fauna?

While he was pondering Susie stripped.

She entered the pool with a loud splash, called, "Come on in! The water's fine!"

She struck out for the opposite bank, her pale body gleaming enticingly under the clear water. Grimes threw off his shirt, stepped out of his shorts and underwear, kicked off his sandals and followed her.

Yes, he thought, the water was fine. And this natural exercise, after the artificial calisthenics aboard the ship, was good. He met Susie in mid-pool. They clung to each other, kissed as they went under. They broke apart, surfaced. She made for a bank where sunlight struck down through the surrounding trees, brightly illumining an area of smooth, brightly green grass. She clambered out, fell to her knees and then rolled over on to her back, legs wide spread.

Grimes joined her, dropped beside her, kissed her again. She was ready, he knew, as he was ready. He mounted her, his chest pillowed on her ample breasts. Her legs came up and over to imprison the lower portion of his body. The sun was warm on his back, her skin was hot below his.

She said sleepily, "This was the best. . . ."

And almost the last time, thought Grimes. Even if he stayed on Joognaan for a few days after the body-change Susie would no longer be Susie. Even her personality would be changing—slowly or not so slowly. Minds may—may?—be supreme but they are, inevitably, conditioned by the bodies that they inhabit.

She said, "I know what you're thinking, John."

"What?" he asked almost guiltily.

"That this is almost the last time for us. But it needn't be. Why shouldn't you change your physical identity too? You can lift *Bronson Star* from where she is now, land her again somewhere where she won't be seen by any incoming spaceships. She'll be a treasure house of metals and machinery for these people. And *you*. . . . You just sit tight with Hodge and myself, just another phoney clone, waiting for the next star tramp to drop in."

Grimes said, "I have to stay me. I have to earn a living the only way that I know how. If I change my identity the Master Astronaut's certificate, issued to John Grimes, is no longer valid. . . ."

She told him, "There'll be plenty of money left—even after we've paid for the body change and our board and lodging here and our passages to wherever. . . ."

Grimes said, "But I have my responsibilities, Susie."

"To the cheese-paring owners of that rustbucket you were baby-sitting? Forget about them. They'll do well enough out of the insurance."

They probably would, thought Grimes. After a suitable lapse of time somebody in far-away London would toll the *Lutine* bell and Lloyd's, admitting that *Bronson Star* was Missing, Presumed Lost, would pay out. And *Little Sister* would be sold to somebody not worthy of her, somebody who, in all probability, would regard her as marketable precious metal rather than a ship.

He said, "I'm sorry. Really sorry. But I have to adhere to my original plan."

She smiled in a rather odd manner.

She whispered, "We'll see about that."

He expected that she would sleep with him again that night and exert all her charm upon him to try to make him change his mind.

But she did not.

Chapter 22

Baarsulimaam called for them quite early the next morning. Grimes was awakened by the alarm that Hodge had set up to give warning of anybody or anything approaching the ship. He hurried up to the control room, looked out and down and saw the steam car standing there and a native getting out from the driver's seat. He opened inner and outer doors by remote control then took the elevator down to the stern. He reached the head of the ramp just as Baarsulimaam was coming up it.

"A good morning to you, Captain Grimes. Forgive my early coming but there was something that I should have told you yesterday. Your friends must not break their fast before the operation."

"Susie won't like that," said Grimes. "But come aboard, Baarsulimaam. Perhaps you will join me in coffee and toast after I have awakened her and Hodge."

"It will be my pleasure."

Baarsulimaam waited in Grimes's day cabin while he called Susie and Hodge. The girl was not at all pleased with the instructions that Grimes passed on to her, said. "I suppose that you'll want to stuff yourself as usual. Well, you can cook your own bloody breakfast."

"I'll do just that," Grimes told her.

Hodge, when he was awakened and told the news, growled, "I suppose I'm allowed to go to the crapper. . . ."

"That, I should imagine," said Grimes, "will be not only allowable but essential."

He went back to his own quarters, made a hasty toilet, dressed and then took the native down to the wardroom. He made coffee and a big tray of toast, found jams and savory spreads—more legacies from the ill-fated royalist expeditionary force. He and Baarsulimaam quite enjoyed the makeshift meal, even when, at the finish of it, they were being watched sulkily by Susie.

The four of them went down to the waiting steam car. Grimes felt a little guilty about leaving the ship unattended but, with the outer airlock door closed and set to open only if the correct code were pushed on the Watchman, as the special button was called, she was safe enough. Susie and Hodge clambered into the back seats of the vehicle, tried to adjust themselves comfortably on a bench that had not been designed for human bodies. Grimes got in beside Balaarsulimaam in the front. It was not the first time that he had ridden in one of these steam cars but, as on that long ago past occasion, he was impressed by the simplicity of the controls. Steam gauge, water gauge, oil fuel gauge. . . . Three wheel valves, one of which radiated heat in spite of the insulation around it. . . . A steering wheel. . . . A lanyard for the whistle. . . . A reversing lever. . . .

The native fed steam into the reciprocating engine, which started at once. He threw the gear lever, which had been in neutral, into reverse, backed away from the ship, turning. Once headed in the right direction he started off along the avenue, soon reaching a good speed.

It was a pleasant enough drive. The sun was just up and bright shafts of light, made visible by the lingering nocturnal mistiness, were striking through the tall, fir-like trees. Once or twice small animals scurried across the road ahead of the car, too fast for the humans to get a good look at them—not that Susie or Hodge were in a mood to be interested in the local zoology. They were both unfed and apprehensive, sitting in glum silence.

Beyond the forest were the fields and beyond the

fields was the city. The low shrubs, with their dark-blue foliage, each laden with ripening yellow fruit, stood ranged in military precision, row after row of them. In comparison—not that comparison was necessary— the city was a jumble, a scattering on the outskirts, a huddle toward the center, of what Grimes had thought of when he first saw them as red-brick igloos. He still thought of them that way. Very few of them were higher than one story; the Joognaanards used ramps rather than staircases and a very large structure is needed to accommodate such a means of ascent from level to level.

Trees and bushes grew in profusion between the domes and even on the domes themselves although the roads were kept well cleared of encroaching vegetation. There was little traffic abroad—the Joognaanards are not early risers—but such few pedestrians as were about, such few drivers and passengers of steam cars who were already going about their various businesses, looked curiously at the three Terrans in Balaarsulimaam's vehicle—but not ill-manneredly so.

They came at last to a large dome almost in the center of the city, one of those standing around a wide, circular plaza. Glistening white letters, looking like the trail left by a drunken snail, shone above its arched doorway.

"The Institution of Medical Science," said Balaarsulimaam proudly. "We go inside. They expect us."

"I don't like this," whispered Hodge.

"It's all right," Susie told him. "If they don't fix us the way we want they don't get paid."

Grimes helped Susie down out of the car. She was carrying a small bag, he noticed. Toilet gear? A nightdress? He did not think, remembering what he had been told of the Joognaan body-changing technique, that she would be needing either.

Balaarsulimaam hopped rather than walked through the archway. Susie and Grimes followed. Hodge brought up the rear. It was dark inside the building but would have been darker without the glowing mantles of the gas lamps. There was an odd, musty smell but the odor was neither dead nor unhealthy. There was the sound of water running somewhere in the inner recesses of the dome.

The native led them unhesitatingly through the maze of corridors, bringing them at last to a room that was surprisingly brightly lit, a large compartment in which was not the profusion of equipment that Grimes, in spite of what he had been told about the Joognaan process, had been expecting. There were two long, deep bathtubs that looked like something out of a Terran museum of bygone household furniture and fittings. There was a low table by each tub. Three white-furred Joognaanards were awaiting the . . . patients? customers? The larger of the trio said something in a mewling voice to Balaarsulimaam, who translated.

"Miss Susie, Mr. Hodge. . . . You are to remove your clothing and get into the baths."

"What's in them?" demanded Hodge.

"It will not harm you, only change you. It is a . . . dissolvent fluid. A nutriment. . . ."

Grimes looked into the tub nearest to himself. Its contents looked innocuous enough, could have been no more than cold consomme, exuded that musty odor which, somehow, signified life rather than decay.

He turned away. Hodge, he saw, had already stripped. He was an excessively hairy man and without his clothing looked more like an ape than ever. Susie was obviously reluctant to disrobe.

"Get a move on!" growled Hodge. "Let's get this over with. What're you so suddenly coy about? Nobody else is wearing a stitch but Grimes—an' he's seen you often enough."

"But they've got fur!" she protested. Then—nastily—"And so have you!"

Nonetheless she stripped, handing her clothing to Grimes.

The head doctor spoke again and again Balaarsulimaam translated.

"Each of you will place the . . . image that you wish

to resemble on the table by your bath. You will look at the image, think hard about it. The thought intensifiers—there is one for each of you—will intensify your thoughts, will help you to control the cells of your body." He turned to Grimes. "In your little ship, the *Adder,* you had an officer who communicated with others like himself by thought. He used the brain of some animal as an intensifier. This is almost the same."

Almost, Grimes thought. But the dog's brain amplifiers of the psionic communication officers were not housed in living bodies but in glass tanks.

"The images, if you are pleased."

Susie took her bag back from Grimes, took from it two solidographs, transparent cubes encasing human figures. Somehow he did not want to look at the one that was to be her model, felt that it would somehow be an invasion of privacy. (She was holding it, too, so that he could not get a good look at it.)

She said, "This is what Hodge will turn into. From frog into prince." She turned the solidograph so that Grimes could see it properly. "It was lucky that I had this with me."

Grimes recognized the handsome young man who was depicted in the cube. He was the hero of a popular TriVi series back on Bronsonia which he had watched on occasion.

Balaarsulimaam took the solidographs from Susie, looked at them curiously and then set them down carefully, one to each of the tables. The head doctor handed to him two flexible tubes. These he passed on to the man and the woman.

He said, "These you must hold in your mouths. All of your bodies, even your heads, must be under. These are . . . are. . . ?"

"Snorkels," supplied Hodge impatiently. "All right, let's get it over with. And I bloody well hope that it's warmer in than out!"

He took one end of his tube in his mouth, clambered into his bath. He arranged the pipe so that it was dan-

gling over the side. Carefully he lowered his hairy body
into the fluid, lay there, completely submerged.

"Must I?" muttered Susie. She shrugged, sending a
ripple down the well-filled skin of her entire body. She
put the end of the snorkel between her full lips, stepped
into the tub. *Like Aphrodite rising from the foam,*
thought Grimes. *In reverse. And if she'd been painted
by Rubens. . . .*

She went down like a full moon setting into a wine-
dark sea. Her body displaced more liquid than that of
Hodge. There was an overflow over the rim of the tub;
it fell to the stone floor with an odd, somehow ominous
slurping noise.

Grimes walked to the bath, looked down. Already
there was a cloudiness, the beginnings of effervescence
among the hairs of her head and those at the base of her
round belly.

He felt sickened and more than a little afraid. What
had he talked her into? He heard the doctor saying
something in his mewing voice.

Balaarsulimaam took his arm, exerted gentle pressure to try to turn him away from the sight of what was
happening to this woman with whom he had made love.

He said, "Better not to stay, Captain. You are too. . . .
involved. Your thoughts might interfere."

"But. . . ."

"Better that you return to your ship. Your friends
are in good hands."

Grimes allowed himself to be led out of the operating
chamber. At the door he paused, looked back for the
last time. There were the two baths, looking ominously
like stone coffins, each with the table beside it, each
with the squatting, black-and-white furred telepath
(telesculptor?) staring fixedly at his faintly gleaming
solidograph cube.

"It will not be long," said Balaarsulimaam. "You are
not to worry."

Grimes allowed himself to be convinced.

Chapter 23

It was very lonely aboard *Bronson Star*.

Balaarsulimaam had come aboard briefly after running Grimes back to the ship, had stayed only for one cup of coffee and then, pleading pressure of business, had returned to the city.

Grimes decided to pass the day with a general spring clean. He started in his own quarters. He decided to clear all the clothing left by Paul and Lania out of his wardrobe and to stow it in the Third Officer's cabin. Not for the first time, while he was so engaged, he made a search for possessions that he had left behind on the occasion of his eviction—his watch, a gold everlasting pen that was a souvenir of *The Far Traveler,* a pocket computer from the same ship, the solidograph of Maggie Lazenby—but without happy result. Paul and Lania must have done something with these things—and Paul and Lania would not be answering any questions any more.

The control room was next to receive his attentions. He checked all the instruments, dusted and polished. He thought of sabotaging the auto-log himself but decided that it would be better to leave this to Hodge; the engineer would be able to make it look like an accident.

Conscious of a good morning's work behind him he went down to the galley, programmed the autochef to cook him a chicken curry lunch. It was palatable enough but had a rather odd flavor. He wondered just what local bird—or reptile?—had made its contribution to the tissue-culture vats when these had been replenished on Porlock.

He smoked a quiet pipe and then went to the farm deck. He had to give Susie full marks for maintenance, he thought. (And what was happening to Susie now? Was that once firmly fleshed body no more than a skeleton submerged in that murky, soupy solution?) Everything was spotlessly clean. The hydroponic tanks were healthily flourishing indoor vegetable plots, the tissue culture and yeast vats, every polishable part and fitting gleaming, could have been scientific equipment in a well-endowed, well-run laboratory rather than an essential component of the ecology of a down-at-heels star tramp. The observation ports of the algae tanks were crystal clear, inside as well as outside. Obviously the aquatic worms that, Susie had told him, she had managed to obtain on Porlock were doing their job. He watched one of the sluglike things browsing on the surface of the glass. He wondered if the same creatures could be used to clean the inside of the Joognaanards' body-sculpture baths. There must, he thought, be some ... *sludge* left over. . . .

He tried hard to switch his train of thought onto a more cheerful track.

He continued his downward progress, through the holds that had, briefly, been troop decks, that still held their tiers of wooden-framed bunks. Some of the fittings were broken—probably due to his violent maneuvers when coming in to land on Dunlevin. He wondered what value all this timber would have on Bronsonia. Would the cost of it be included in the salvage award? If any?

The engine compartments were next. Hodge, Grimes decided, was not as house-proud as Susie. The only things polished were things that had to be polished, the faces of gauges and the like. There was a thin film of oil over everything else. But there was no untidiness and everything seemed to be in perfect order.

Everything, Grimes hoped, would continue that way;

the last leg of his voyage must be made without an engineer.

His inspection ended, he stood at the open airlock door, looking out at the somber forest, staring along the white road that led to the city. There were no vehicles on it.

He returned to his quarters and tried to pass the time watching the playmaster. He could not find a spool in the ship's not very extensive library that was capable of holding his attention.

He had an early dinner and rather too much to drink and then retired.

His sleep was nightmare haunted; absurdly fat skeletons chased him through his dreams.

The next morning Balaarsulimaam came out to the ship.

Before Grimes could ask the question he answered it. "All goes well, Captain. The rebuilding process has begun."

"And there are no problems?"

"There are no problems." Balaarsulimaam made the high-pitched whinny that passed for a laugh among his people. "Perhaps when you see your friends you will consent to have your ears diminished. That will be without charge."

"No thank you," said Grimes.

Grimes escorted the native up to his quarters, got out bottle, ice and glasses.

"How soon," he asked, "before Susie and Hodge are able to resume a normal life?" He was painfully aware from the burning of his prominent ears that he was blushing. "I would like a little time with her before I lift off. . . ."

"I did guess how it is with you and the young lady. *We*, unlike you Terrans, do have only one sexual mate during our lifetime and so do not suffer from the problems that seem always to afflict your people. From what I learned during my voyage to Earth I am of the opinon that you flit from female to female like a *carnidal* from *bilaan* to *bilaan.* . . ."

"I'm sorry that you don't approve," said Grimes stiffly.

"I neither approve nor not approve. But do not worry. You shall sip once more from the sugared cup."

Chapter 24

Grimes did not anticipate that Susie and Hodge would be returning to the ship at night. Had he known, he would have stayed up to welcome them—or he would have made sure, before retiring, that the radar alarm was switched on. As a matter of fact he did remember that he had failed to actuate this warning device but he was already in bed, and drowsy. On this planet, he told himself, there was no need to take precautions against nocturnal attack. Furthermore the airlock door was closed and only the three humans knew the code that would open it from the outside. The last that Balaarsulimaam had told him was that he would be allowed to see the girl and the engineer the following day. He fell asleep wondering what she would look like, which star of the Bronsonian entertainment screens she would have remodeled herself to resemble.

He fell asleep without having to work hard at it.

He did not dream—although at first he thought that it was a dream that he had awakened to.

The light in his bedroom came on.

He opened his eyes, blinked muzzily and then stared at the woman who stood just inside the doorway. She was quite naked, slim, fine featured, auburn haired. There was a beauty spot, a mole, over her small, firm left breast. This minor blemish seemed unusually distinct.

He was dreaming. He *knew* that he was dreaming. Maggie Lazenby could not possibly be here, on this world.

(But she might be, he thought. She just might be.

Perhaps a Survey Service ship, with herself among the officers, had landed. Perhaps he had slept through the cacophony of its descent.)

Maggie (Maggie?) walked slowly into the cabin. She seemed to have lost the grace with which she usually moved and the smile that curved her wide mouth was not quite right.

(This *is* a dream, Grimes thought, oddly relieved.)

The scent of her, the muskiness of a sexually aroused human female, was *wrong,* wrong yet familiar. And her skin was too pale.

(But I don't want to wake up just yet, he thought.)

She came to his bed, stooped to plant a kiss (it tasted wrong) on his mouth. Her erect nipples brushed his bare chest. She straightened, turned slowly around until she faced him again. (Maggie would have pirouetted.)

She asked, "What do you think of the new *me,* John?"

He gasped, "Susie!"

"On stage live, in person, singing and dancing." She stared down at his face. "Aren't you *pleased?*"

He said weakly, "It's a surprise. . . ."

"But aren't you *pleased?*"

He was not. He realized then that, however much he might philander, his essential loyalties lay to one woman only—and Susie most certainly was not she.

"Aren't you *pleased?*"

Suddenly anger supplanted all other emotions. He growled, "So that's where my solidograph of Maggie went. *You* stole it. . . ."

"I did not. Lania threw it out after she caught Paul leering at it."

"You must have known that I valued it. You should have given it to me."

"And had her looking at us from the top of your desk every time that we made love? With you making odious comparisons and me knowing that you were doing just that? If it's any consolation to you, I used her as my model only because there was nothing else around—unless you count that tawdry calendar in the

Third Mate's cabin. In any case, whose bright idea was it that I should have a body change?"

"But you aren't Maggie. . . ."

"I know bloody well I'm not. And Hodge isn't Trevor Carradine, but he looks like him and that'll be good enough for me. This was to have been a sort of thank-you-for-everything, farewell session, John—but you've ruined it." She snatched the sheet from off his body. "Look at you! When I came in you were making a tent but *now*. . . . Like one of those slime-eating slugs in the algae tanks. . . ."

"But. . . ."

"You've said enough, John. I'll go where I'm appreciated. Hodge has been trying hard to get some place with me ever since they dragged us out of their tubs and rinsed us off."

"But. . . ."

"But we have the same father? So bloody what? Some planets get all hot and bothered about incest, some don't. And in any case we're starting afresh with brand new identities.

"So this is good-bye, John. Hodge is wiping the auto-log for you now and all that I have to do is to pick up the money from the safe in my office. We'll leave you to your sweet dreams of Maggie—what a name!—and you can get off this world and back to your precious *Little Sister* as soon as you like.

"Good-bye."

As she turned to go Grimes jumped out of the bed, caught her by the slim shoulders, pulled her back to him. His erection grew again. No matter what or whom she looked like, no matter how much weight she had shed, she felt like Susie. She did not struggle as he forced her round to face him, as he pressed his mouth to hers. With the full frontal contact there was only the faintest hint of the girl that she had been—but it was enough.

As long as he kept his eyes closed.

He took her brutally on the disordered bed and she

did not resist. She was there too and she made him fully aware of it.

When he was fully spent and she sated, she slithered from under him, tottered rather than walked to the door. She turned, supporting herself with one long, slim arm on the door frame.

She said, "All right. This *is* good-bye. I'm glad that it was with a bang and not with a whimper—and I'm sorry that you aren't staying here to take your chances with us. . . . You still could. . . ."

He said, "I'm sorry that you can't come back to Bronsonia with me. I could use a purser aboard my own ship, when I get her back. . . ."

She said, "You just used a purser. Oh, well. Good-bye, good luck and all that. And give my love to *Little Sister*."

He said, regretting the words as soon as he had uttered them, "And give mine to your half brother."

She called him a nasty, sarcastic bastard and then was gone.

Chapter 25

He did not expect to see her again but she came out to the ship, accompanied by Balaarsulimaam and three other Joognaanards, before he lifted off for the voyage back to Bronsonia. She was dressed in one of Lania's black uniforms; her own clothing would not have fit her now. She was carrying a large parcel wrapped in a square of gaudily patterned cloth.

The natives, too, were bearing gifts—baskets of fruit, bottles of *talaagra*.

Balaarsulimaam said, "It has been good to see you again, Captain Grimes. And worry not, your friends will be in good hands. And if ever you should wish your ears remodeled. . . ."

"Thank you," said Grimes. "I'll remember. And I hope that when I come here again I shall be able to enjoy a longer stay."

After handshaking, the natives tactfully hopped out of the day cabin, leaving him alone with Susie.

She grinned rather lopsidedly. She said, handing him the parcel, "Here's something to remember me by, John. No, don't open it now." She kissed him, rather clumsily; that package was between them. "Good-bye. Or *au revoir?* I'll see you out on the Rim Worlds, perhaps. Who knows?"

She turned and left him. He heard the whine of the elevator as it carried his visitors down to the airlock. He went up to Control, watched from a viewport Susie and the others walking to the waiting steam car and then standing alongside it. She waved. He waved back although it was doubtful that she would be able to see the salute.

He busied himself with last-minute preparations, sealing the ship and satisfying himself that all life-support systems were fully operational. No pilot lights, he noted, glowed on the otherwise featureless cube of the autolog. So Hodge (he hoped) had kept his promise, so there would be no record of the deviation. He took the command seat, strapped himself in. The inertial drive grumbled into life at his first touch on the controls. She drove up, slowly at first and then faster and faster. It was a lift-off without incident, with everything functioning smoothly.

So it went on and, after this smooth departure, *Bronson Star* was, before long, on trajectory for her home world. Grimes made sure that all alarms were functioning and then went down to his quarters. He uncorked one of the bottles of gift wine, poured himself a glass. After he had finished it he poured another, but let it stand untouched on the coffee table while he unwrapped Susie's present. There were two solidographs in the parcel. One was that of Maggie Lazenby. The other. . . .

No, it was not a solidograph.

It was a squat bottle of clear glass, filled with some transparent fluid. Suspended in it was a tiny, naked woman, full-bodied, with blonde hair and pale skin, a miniature Susie. And she was—somehow—alive. (Or were her movements due only to the way in which the container was being turned around in his hands?) A rather horrid thought came to him. Susie, while immersed in the body-sculpture bath, had lost surplus tissue. And what had happened to those unwanted cells?

But, he rationalized, this was, after all, a quite precious gift. Men have treasured locks of hair from the heads of their lovers. (And locks of hair from other parts of their bodies.) Men have gone into battle wearing their ladies' favors, articles of intimate feminine apparel still carrying the body scents of their original owners. This present, after all, was the same in principle but to a far greater degree.

He put the bottle down on the table. It vibrated in harmony with the vibrations of the inertial drive. It looked as though the tiny Susie were performing a belly dance.

And was this altogether due to the vibrations?

It must be, he thought, although the only way to be sure would be to break the bottle and to remove its living or preserved contents for examination. And he had no intention of doing that. He did not wish to have a piece of decomposing female flesh on his hands and the thought of feeding what was, after all, a piece of Susie into the ship's waste disposal and conversion system was somehow abhorrent.

He raised his glass in salute to the tiny Susie, drank. He raised it again to the solidograph of Maggie. He was sorry that neither of them was aboard to keep him company on this voyage. He had never been especially lonely in *Little Sister* but she was only a small vessel. In *Bronson Star,* a relatively big ship, there were far too many empty spaces.

The voyage wore on.

Grimes rehearsed, time and time again, the edited version of the story of *Bronson Star's* voyagings that he would submit to the authorities, wrote the first, second and subsequent drafts of his report. He prepared the Number Two boat for ejection; he was sorry that he did not have the materials at hand to manufacture a time bomb, but the possibility of such a small craft being picked up and found empty was very slight. He admired Hodge's thoroughness regarding a simulated breakdown of the Mannschenn Drive. Essential wiring had been ripped out, had been replaced with patched lengths of cable, installed with scant regard for appearance, obviously the work of a ham-handed amateur mechanic.

Meanwhile he enjoyed his meals, was inclined to drink rather too much (he had found the mess sergeant's formula for the perversion of the autochef), exercised religiously to keep his weight down and set up war games in the chart tank to exercise his mind.

The solidograph and the pseudo-solidograph he did not stow away in a convenient drawer; the representations of the two women stood on his desk, facing each other. He often wondered what they would say to each other if ever they met in actuality.

Chapter 26

All would have been well had the Mannschenn Drive not broken down in actuality; that makeshift wiring installed by Hodge had been rather too makeshift. Grimes was not in his quarters when it happened; he was in the control room with the Battle of Wittenhaven set up in the chart tank, trying to make it come out differently from the way that it had in historical fact.

He suddenly realized that Commodore van der Bergen's squadron, as represented by red sparks in the screen, was in full retreat instead of closing in for the kill. Testily he manipulated the controls but the knurled knobs seemed to have a will of their own, were turning the wrong way under his fingers.

The Manschenn Drive, he thought. *"The governor. . . ."*

Obviously it had ceased to function and equally obviously the temporal precession field was building up to a dangerous level. There should have been an automatic cut-off of power to the drive but the fail-safe device had just . . . failed. (It usually did; there were so many paradoxes involved that even a simple on-off switch would do the wrong thing.)

Grimes hoped that the remote controls were still operable. He fought his way to the command chair; it seemed to him that he was having to climb up a deck tilted at a forty-five-degree angle, that he was almost having to swim through an atmosphere congealed to the consistency of treacle. (Illusion it may have been but he was sweating profusely.) The command chair, with the essential ship-handling controls set in its wide arms,

119

seemed to recede to a remote distance, to dwindle, as he struggled toward it. And then, with a bone-bruising collision, he was falling over it.

He stabbed, almost blindly, with a stiffened index finger, hoping that he was hitting the right button. It was like spearing a fish at the bottom of a clear stream and trying to allow for refraction.

The thin, high Mannschenn whine deepened in pitch from the almost supersonic to the normally sonic, deepened further still to a low humming, ceased. With an almost audible snap, perspective and color resumed normality. Outside the viewports the stars were once again hard, multi-hued points of light in the interstellar blackness.

He wasted no time looking out at them. He hurried from the control room, took the elevator down to the engine compartments. (Now that he was alone in the ship the cage was always where he wanted it.) Blue smoke still lingered in the Mannschenn Drive room, in spite of the forced ventilation. There was a stink of burned insulation. The cause of the trouble was obvious enough. The protective coating of one of the wires installed by Hodge had chafed through and the wire itself had been melted by the arc between it and sharp-edged metal. The power supply to the governor had been cut. In theory this should have resulted in a loss of power to the complexity of ever-precessing gyroscopes but Hodge had done his best to convey the impression of a rewiring job having been done by somebody without much of a clue as to what he was doing.

Grimes found a length of wire in the spares locker. He removed the two ends of burned cable, substituted the replacement. He went to the local control switchboard and —wondering if he were doing the right thing —switched on. He heard the low hum as the rotors began to spin, heard the noise rise in pitch. The green indicator light at which he was staring took on the appearance of a luminous fire opal, seemed to expand to the likeness of some great, blazing planet toward which he was plunging.

Then, suddenly, it was no more than a little, innocuous emerald light.

He turned to look briefly (very briefly), to stare too long at those tumbling, ever-precessing, always-on-the-verge-of-vanishing rotors is to court disaster. All seemed to be well.

He returned to the control room to check the ship's position by means of Carlotti bearings and then to make the necessary adjustment of trajectory.

He told himself, *I could do with a drink.*

He went down to his day cabin.

He noticed the smell at once; it was the same mustiness that he had sniffed in the . . . operating theatre back on Joognaan. He looked at his desk top. The solidograph of Maggie still stood there but the bottle in which the likeness of Susie had been suspended was now no more than a scattering of jagged shards. Fluid had dripped from the deck on to the carpet, staining it badly. Among the broken glass was a formless pink blob.

He felt a stab of regret.

So this, he thought, was the last of Susie. It was a great pity that she had not given him a conventional solidograph; such a portrait would have survived the breakage of its container. He sighed audibly—and it seemed to him that the wide mouth of the miniature Maggie, standing proudly in her transparent cube, was curved in a derisive smile.

He looked closely at the mess on the desk, being careful not to touch it. He did not know what the fluid in the bottle had been or what effect it would have on the skin of his fingers. He prodded the fleshy blob cautiously with a pen from the rack, turned it over. Yes, there was the hair where hair should have been, and that little streak of scarlet must have been the mouth and those two, tiny pink spots the nipples. . . . Perhaps if he put it into another container it would regain its shape. . . . But in what fluid? Distilled water? Alcohol?

He could imagine it—her?—suspended in a medium

that would become murkier and murkier, with parts of her dropping off perhaps. . . .

It was a horrid thought.

He went through to his bathroom to collect a generous handful of tissues, returned to gingerly pick up the amorphous blob of . . . flesh? pseudo-flesh? and then carried it to the toilet bowl. Oddly, he felt no sentimental regrets as he flushed it away. It was too ugly, was no more than an obscene mess. The broken glass he disposed of down the inorganic waste chute.

When he was finished he noticed dark moisture on the carpet under the closed door of his grog locker. He investigated. The remaining bottles of the wine from Joognaan had shattered. He felt a surge of relief. Until this moment the frightening suspicion had lurked in the back of his mind that when the temporal precession field intensified the homunculus had somehow become really alive, had burst out of its glass prison from the inside. But it had been the painfully high pitch of the sound emanating from the Drive that had done the damage; Joognaanard glassware, all too obviously, was not as tough as that normally supplied to spaceships.

Chapter 27

After that near disaster with the Mannschenn Drive Grimes instituted a routine of daily inspections. There were so many things to go wrong in a ship that was long past her youth and with only himself, a not very good mechanic, to fix them. He spent much time on the farm deck; its flora did more than provide him with food. They purified and regenerated the atmosphere that he breathed, cycled and recycled the water that he drank and washed in.

He noticed that the population of aquatic worms in the algae vats was diminishing. This was no real cause for concern; their only function was to keep the inner surfaces of the observation ports clean. Still, he missed them. They were, like himself, motile organisms. They were company of a sort.

And then, one ship's day, he glimpsed through a now merely translucent inspection port something swimming. It looked too large to be one of the sluglike things and its color was wrong. Perhaps, thought Grimes, the aquatic worms had mutated; this was unlikely, however, they were exposed to a no greater level of radiation in the ship than in their natural environment. Or—this was more likely—the worms brought aboard on Porlock had been a larval form. What would the adults be like? There had been a suggestion of fins or other appendages about the creature that he had briefly seen.

He spent more and more time on the farm deck. Quite often now he was catching brief glimpses of these new swimmers. He wanted a better look at them. He knew that bio-chemists in really big ships, the ones, naval or mercantile, that carried a multiplicity of technicians on their books, had a technique for cleaning inspection ports from the inside and that this method was also used by catering officers in smaller vessels. The tank tops had little, removable hatches directly above the side inspection ports. There was a squeegee with a handle of just the right length that could be manipulated from the outside.

He finally found a squeegee. It didn't look as though it had been used for a long time. Then, from the engineroom stores, he brought up a small shifting spanner. The nuts holding down the hatch lid were very tight; finally, at the cost of barked knuckles, he removed them. He lifted the hinged cover. He realized then why biochemists and catering officers did not relish the port cleaning job, preferring to employ some lowly organism such as the aquatic worms to do it for them. The stench that gusted out from the opening was almost palpable.

Grimes retched, retreated with more haste than dignity. Before he carried on with the job he would have to find or improvise a breathing mask. He recalled having seen a facepiece with attached air bottle and piping in the engine-room stores.

He was about to go to fetch it when an alarm bell sounded so, instead of making his way aft, he hurried back up to Control.

It was not a real emergency.

The mass proximity indicator had picked up a target at a range of one thousand kilometers. A ship, thought Grimes, peering into the blackness of the three-dimensional screen at the tiny, bright spark. He watched it, set up extrapolated trajectories. The stranger would pass, he estimated, within fifty kilometers of *Bronson Star*. There was no danger of collision, not that two ships running under interstellar drive could ever collide unless their temporal precession rates were exactly synchronized.

Grimes switched on the Carlotti transceiver. Presumably *Bronson Star* was showing up in the other vessel's MPI screen. Almost immediately a voice came from the speaker.

"*Doberman* calling passing vessel, *Doberman* calling passing vessel. What ship, please? What ship? Come in, please. Come in."

He was tempted to talk to the Dog Star liner but refrained. He would adhere to his original intention, not to use the Carlotti for transmission until just prior to arrival at Bronsonia. His story would be that he had feared pursuit by units of the Dunlevin Navy and had been reluctant to betray his position. If he now exchanged greetings with *Doberman* it would be known that he was approaching Bronsonia from Joognaan, not from Dunlevin.

"*Doberman* calling passing vessel. . . ."

What if he replied, wondered Grimes, using a false name for his ship? It had been so long, too long, since he had talked with anybody. His vocal chords must be atrophying. . . . But the apparently harmless deceit could lead, just possibly, to too many complications.

"*Doberman* calling passing vessel. . . ." Then, in an obvious aside to some superior, "Probably some poverty-stricken tramp, sir. . . . Too poor or too lousy to afford MPI. . . ."

Then the reply in a much fainter voice, "Or somebody who doesn't want his whereabouts known."

"Not very likely, sir. There aren't any pirates around these days."

"Aren't there, Mr. Tibbs? What about Shaara rogue queens? I heard that the famous Commander Grimes had a set-to with one not long since."

"*Grimes!* As you know, sir, I've a commission in the Reserve. . . ."

"I know it all right, Tibbs! At times you seem to think that you're First Lieutenant of a Constellation Class cruiser rather than Second Mate of a star tramp!"

"Let me finish, sir. I did most of my last drill attached to Lindisfarne Base and people still talked about Grimes, even though it's some time since he resigned his

commission. Some of the things he got away with. . . .
He was little better than a pirate himself!"

"So, just as I've been telling you, there *are* pirates.
. . . But our unknown friend's not attempting to close
us. Can't be either a Shaara rogue queen or the notorious
Grimes. . . ."

There is nothing more frustrating than listening to
a conversation about oneself and being unable to speak
up in self-defense. Bad-temperedly Grimes switched
off the Carlotti. Then he became aware that the aroma
from the farm deck was being distributed throughout
the ship by the ventilation system. He thought wrily,
It's not only my name that stinks.

He hurried down to the engine-room stores, found
a breathing mask and returned to the farm deck. He
used the squeegee to clean off the inspection port—a
job rather more awkward than he had anticipated—and
then replaced the little hatch. He peered intently
through the now-transparent glass but saw nothing—
neither the original aquatic worms nor their successors.

Perhaps, he thought, the adults could not adapt to
life in a ship's algae vat as well as the larval form. Perhaps they had died. Perhaps their decomposition had
contributed to that horrendous stink, much worse than
could be expected from the normal processing of sewage and organic garbage.

He hoped that the air-conditioning system would
not take too long about cleansing the foul taint from
Bronson Star's atmosphere.

Chapter 28

For a while after his cleaning of the inspection port Grimes avoided the farm deck; in spite of the valiant efforts of the extractor fans the stink lingered. It was one of those smells the mere memory of which can trigger off a retching fit. It had penetrated even the breathing mask that Grimes had worn.

He relied upon the control room instrumentation to keep him well informed as to the well-being of tissue cultures, yeasts, algae and the plants in the hydroponic tanks. He seemed to have no immediate cause for worry but he knew that he would have to procure fresh supplies of meat and vegetables; the ready-use cold store that was an adjunct to the autochef was running low. And there were one or two recipes that he wished to program involving fresh tomatoes. Susie, putting the hydroponic tanks into full commission during the brief stay on Porlock, had planted a few vines; she, Grimes recalled, had expressed her great liking for that fruit. Some must be ready now for the plucking.

He had sealed the farm deck off from the rest of the ship. Entering the compartment he had the breathing mask ready to slip on in an instant but it was not required. The air still held a very faint hint of the original stink but it could be ignored.

Grimes went at once to the tank with the tomato vines. There were some fruit but they were small, green, inedible. This was strange. He was sure that he had seen, the last time that he had visited the farm deck, a fine crop that was already yellow, that must surely ripen to scarlet lusciousness within a very few days.

127

Perhaps they had fallen and rotted—but there was no trace of skin or pips on the loosely packed fibers that formed an artificial soil. Yet he could see from the vines that fruit had been there on the stems.

Odd, he thought. *Very odd. . . .*

He made a round of the hydroponic tanks. He discovered no further anomalies. He went to look at the yeast vats. These were covered only with wire mesh. Over one of the vats the fine netting was torn. Had it always been so? Grimes could not remember. Was this old or recent damage? He did not know. The surface of the spongy mass inside the vat looked undisturbed—but the yeast used as a food source in spaceships is a remarkably fast growing organism.

There had been, he remembered, a certain carelessness regarding the airlock door while the ship had been on Joognaan. Something might well have gotten aboard there. A hungry animal would very soon find its way to a source of food. So it—whatever it was—liked tomatoes and, for lack of anything tastier, could feed on yeast. Apart from the fruit it had not touched any of the tank-grown vegetation which indicated that it was more carnivore than herbivore; yeast is a good meat substitute.

Grimes did not begrudge the animal an occasional meal; with only himself aboard the ship there was food aplenty. But animals running loose in human habitations are apt to foul and to destroy far more than they eat. He continued his investigations. He discovered that it—the filthy beast!—had defecated in the tray in which otherwise promising lettuces had been growing.

He had been looking forward to a green salad.

Poisoned bait? he asked himself.

No.

The thing had not been house trained and could hardly be blamed for its use of the lettuce bed as a latrine. In any case (a) there were probably no poisons on board and (b) even if they were they would probably be ineffective against a Joognaanard life form.

A trap?

Yes.

He went down to the engine-room workshop. He found a metal tool box with hinged lid, removed its contents, washed it in hot, soapy water to remove all taint of oil, made sure that the hinges worked freely. The lid had a snap catch so that the box could be opened only from the outside.

The trap would be a simple one; just a metal rod to prop up the lid, the bait—but what bait?—secured to the bottom of the upright. A sharp tug on this should bring the lid slamming down.

He thought—judging from the size of the droppings—that the box would be big enough. If it were not the stowaway would at least get a nasty headache.

Grimes was no electrician but thought that he would be able to fix a cord to the lid that, snapping tight when it fell, would switch on the alarm which, when not being so misused, was supposed to indicate that the pump maintaining the flow of macerated garbage and sewage into the algae vats had stopped.

After all that work he felt ready for his dinner. He trated himself to steak, rare, with French-fried potatoes (these latter actually no more than processed and molded starch) and a bottle of the mess sergeant's rough red. He would have had grilled tomatoes with the meal if it, whatever it was, had not gotten to the vines first.

He saved a piece of bloody steak to bait the trap, took it down to the farm deck to set everything up.

He was no sooner back in his own quarters than he heard the alarm bell ringing in the control room.

Chapter 29

He hurried down to the farm deck. He jumped out
of the elevator cage, ran through the open doorway of
the food production compartment. He saw things—
small, active animals—milling around the sprung trap.
He caught only a glimpse of them, received a con-
fused impression of pale skin and waving limbs as
they scattered at his approach, scurrying to hide behind and under tanks and vats.

He approached the tool box cautiously. The lid had
not fallen all the way down; whatever had displaced the
upright was caught half in, half out. The hindquarters of
the hapless little beast were no more than a bloody mess
with most of the flesh ripped from the fragile bones.
By the looks of what was left it had been a quadruped
of some kind.

Grimes conquered his revulsion, opened the lid.
What was inside was undamaged. He knew what it was
even before he lifted it out carefully and turned it over.
He looked down in horror at the contorted features of
a dead, miniature Susie. At last he put the mutilated
body, all of it, back into the box, shut and secured the
lid. He carried the container out of the farm deck and
then up to his quarters, making sure that all doors
were closed behind him. He put the box on his desk
then poured himself a stiff drink and sat down to think
things over.

He remembered how he had flushed that original
homunculus down his toilet, thinking that it was dead.
Its flesh would have been macerated together with
sewage and other organic garbage before being pumped

into the algae vats. He remembered, then, how he had told Balaarsulimaam about clones. This information must have been passed on to the Joognaanard body sculptors who, making use of it, incorporating it with their own techniques, had produced, to Susie's instructions, what was, in effect, a mini-clone. (That name would do as well as any.) He did not think that Susie's motivations had been malicious. She could not have anticipated that the bottle would be broken, that its contents would be disposed of as they had been.

One thing was certain; he must not dispose of the remains of this Susie as he had disposed of the remains of the original one. There would have to be a proper spaceman's funeral, the ejection out through the airlock of the body.

But that would have to wait. Before any mass is ejected from an interstellar ship the drive must be stopped; failure to observe this precaution almost inevitably leads to disaster. Nobody has yet returned to tell what it is like to fall into a self-generated black hole. So the most sensible thing to do, thought Grimes, would be to wait until he had disposed of all the mini-Susies and then to consign the accumulation of cadavers to space in one operation.

He told himself disgustedly, *You're a cold-blooded bastard, Grimes!*

But even though he had liked the original Susie, even loved her in his fashion, he felt no affection for her . . . progeny? Yes, that word would have to do. He remembered the high-pitched, vicious chitterings that he had heard when he interrupted that macabre feast. He did not have to open the lid of the tool box to see again the tattered ruin of what had been a shapely rump and pair of legs. For all their human appearance these clones—mini-clones? pseudo-clones?—were only mindless but dangerous carnivores.

Too, he had to look after himself.

He would have his story to tell when finally he returned to Bronsonia—a story concocted as much for the protection of Susie and Hodge as for his own benefit. And would that tale hold water if *Bronson Star,* returned to her rightful owners, were found to be infested with tiny humanoids, each one the image of a woman wanted by the authorities for the crime of skyjacking?

There would be questions, very awkward questions, asked.

So. . . .

How to disinfect the ship in the time remaining to him before planetfall?

Poison would have been one answer—*if* he had been able to lay his hands on any. But even if he had there would have been the possibility—the probabality—that the things would die in inaccessible places.

Traps?

He had tried the idea once and hadn't liked the end results.

Starvation?

The things were meat eaters. They had disposed of the aquatic worms in the algae tanks. They had helped themselves from one of the yeast vats. They had at least half eaten one of their own number.

Suppose, he thought, he cleaned out the yeast vats; these, with only a wire-mesh cover to protect their contents, were far too accessible. The tissue-culture and algae vats were safe enough from depredation, however. The hydroponic tanks? There was food there if the homunculi could adapt to a vegetarian diet. Already they had eaten the tomatoes. (*And befouled the lettuces* . . . thought Grimes sourly.) So the "market garden" would have to go. Life-support systems would continue to function nonetheless. The algae were quite capable of purifying water and regenerating atmosphere —especially when there was only one man (one man and an unknown number of mini-women) to maintain. And there was an ample supply of assorted meats. Several kilograms of those, just to be on the safe side, could be transferred from the growing vats to the galley cold stores.

And then. . . .

Possibly cannibalism would bring about a reduction of numbers, although indications were that this did not occur unless the victim was already dead. But the process might take too long.

Grimes visualized a trail of scraps of meat—not large pieces, only enough to stimulate the appetite— leading from the farm deck, down the spiral staircase around the axial shaft to the boat bay. Inside the boat would be the real bait. When the little horrors were feeding, Grimes would seal the boat bay, shut down the Mannschenn Drive, eject the boat (which had to be gotten rid of in any case as corroboration of his fictional account of the voyage) and then resume passage.

There was very little chance that the boat would ever be picked up.

If it were, of course, it would be discovered that it came from *Bronson Star* and the salvagers would be puzzled by the tiny but apparently human corpses.

But then—if it ever happened—Grimes would be a long, long way from Bronsonia. He might even be dead of old age.

In any case it was nothing to worry about. But the immediate situation most certainly was.

Chapter 30

Before commencing operations on the farm deck, Grimes armed himself, belting on one of the projectile pistols left behind by the Dunlevin royalists. He hoped that he would not be obliged to use it; there would be far too great a risk of shattering vital equipment. A shotgun would have been a far better weapon in these circumstances but he possessed neither the tools nor the expertise to modify the pistols or their ammunition.

The first job was to empty the yeast vats, using the scoop that had been designed for that purpose. He shoveled the musty-smelling stuff into whatever containers he could muster—buckets, plastic boxes from which he had emptied small stores, a couple of big mixing bowls from the galley. These he carried out to the waiting elevator cage for transport down to the after airlock.

It was hard enough work for one not accustomed to it and it took longer than it should have done. He *knew* that he was being watched and he paused frequently to look around, hand on the butt of the holstered pistol, every time that he caught a flicker of movement out of the corner of his eye.

But at last the job was finished and he rode down and aft surrounded by tottering stacks of boxes, buckets and basins. He carried the containers into the airlock chamber, getting himself thoroughly smeared with yeast in the process. He realized, belatedly, that the work would have been far less heavy if he had thought to reduce acceleration.

He returned to the farm deck. *They* must have

heard him coming. They boiled out of the yeast vats, where they had been scrabbling for the last scraps of sustenance, just as he came through the door. Most of them bolted for cover but two of them ran straight for him. They were tiny, naked, unarmed—but he was afraid of them. He pulled the pistol, fired. The reports were thunderous, reverberating from metal surfaces. The leading assailant was . . . splattered. The second one came on. Grimes fired again, and again. He saw an arm torn from the doll-like figure—but still it came on.

It jumped. Its sharp little teeth closed on his right wrist. He screamed, dropped the gun, and with his left hand caught the pseudo-clone about its waist, felt his fingers sink into the soft flesh. It chittered shrilly. He pulled, felt his own skin and flesh rip as he dragged the vicious little being away from him. He threw it down to the deck, stamped on it, feeling and hearing the splintering of bones.

He avoided looking at the mess as he stooped to recover his pistol.

He glared around but saw no indications of further attack.

Grimes retreated from the farm deck, making sure that the door was tightly shut after him and could be opened only from the outside. Nursing his bleeding wrist he made his way to the ship's dispensary where he treated what was, after all, only a minor flesh wound with antibiotic spray and newskin dressing.

Then, back in his quarters, he put on a spacesuit. He felt that he would need armor to protect him when he continued his work. He returned to the scene of the incident, thinking that the first job would be to dispose of the bodies. But there were no bodies. Not a trace remained of them—no bones, not even the faintest smear of blood on the deck. Cautiously, alert for further assaults, he went to the yeast vats. The interior of these seemed to have been, quite literally, licked clean.

So they had been hungry, he thought. The little swine would be hungrier yet before he was finished with them. . . .

He cleared the hydroponic tanks of all their vegetation and turned off the irrigation/nutrition system lest fresh growth develop from some overlooked rootlet. He took the plants down to the after airlock where he stowed them with the containers of yeast. Finally he opened one of the tissue-culture vats to take from it what meat he would require for the remainder of the voyage. He feared that the smell of the raw beef would be too much for the homunculi, that they would emerge from their hiding places in a mass attack. Very faintly through his helmet he could hear their high-pitched squealings. He worked by touch rather than by sight, endeavoring to keep the entire farm deck under observation, ready to drop the sharp-edged scoop and to draw his pistol at the first sign of trouble.

But he saw nothing and finally withdrew from the farm deck, with his dripping load, without being molested.

Chapter 31

Just how human were the mini-Susies? wondered Grimes as he—in spite of everything—enjoyed his dinner of rare roast beef. What was their psychological makeup—if they had one? As he chewed the almost raw meat he thought about cannibalism, remembered what he had read about that deplorable practice. It was said to be an addictive vice, that a taste for long pig, once acquired, drove its possessor to gruesome lengths to keep it satisfied. There had been cannibals living in countries on Old Earth in which there had been no shortage of meat from the lower animals but who had still devoured their own kind to gratify their obscene appetites. That family living in a remote part of Scotland, for example, who finally had been hunted down and executed by one of the Stuart kings. . . .

Inevitably the homunculi would reduce their numbers by cannibalism until there would be a solitary survivor. But how many of them were there? How long would the auto-extermination program take? Grimes did not want to delay his arrival back at Bronsonia for too many days, if at all. He wanted to get back to that world as soon as possible, while there was still a chance of saving *Little Sister* from the auctioneer's gavel.

So he would have to continue with his original plan of luring the things into the boat that would also be a trap, the boat that he would then eject to explain the absence of Hodge and Susie from the ship. But what if they—those who still survived—had developed such a taste for human—he supposed that it was human—flesh that they scorned tank-grown beef? But, he reasoned, once their numbers had diminished it would be less easy for them to catch and kill each other. They would be continually ravenous. A hungry man will enjoy food that normally he would sneer at.

In any case, Grimes didn't want to go near the farm deck again until he absolutely had to.

He passed the time pottering.

He stopped the Mannschenn Drive briefly so that he could eject the garbage, the yeast and the vegetation, from the airlock. He took his time about resetting trajectory. He carried out maintenance on the ship's boats, even the one that he intended to sacrifice; after all, something might happen to necessitate a hasty abandonment of ship. He set up a pistol range in one of the holds and experimented with the small arms ammunition, trying to make bullets that would disintegrate as soon as leaving the muzzle, the fragments spreading like shot. One hand gun was ruined when this breakup occurred too soon. He gave the idea away. There would be far too great a risk of a weapon hopelessly jammed just when he most needed it.

He set up and baited his trap.

He cut one piece of raw meat from the cold store into very small pieces, hardly more than crumbs, laid a trail from the door to the farm deck down to the bay in which No. 1 Boat sat in readiness; he had decided on using this lifecraft as it was the nearest. A larger piece of meat he put in the boat itself. Unfortunately *Bronson Star* was deficient in the telltale devices common in larger ships such as passenger liners. There was no closed-circuit TV to give control-room coverage of every compartment. Grimes would have to open the farm deck door and then take the elevator down to boat bay level. He hoped that he would be able to lurk there unobserved, hidden by a convenient curve in the lateral alleyway, until his victims were all in the bay if not in the boat itself. Then, using local controls, he would close the door. This accomplished he would have to hurry back to Control to shut down the Mannschenn Drive. After this the outer door of the boat bay could be opened and atmosphere, boat and mini-Susies ejected explosively.

He decided against wearing space armor; it hampered his movements too much. He wore a belt with holstered pistol, however. He sat and smoked for a while, waiting for the pieces of meat to thaw properly, to start exuding their effluvium. He looked at the solidograph of Maggie.

He thought ironically, *Soon you'll have no competition. . . .*

He looked at the tool box still standing on the desk, his first attempt at a trap. He had quite forgotten to do anything about it and its grisly contents. It would have to wait now.

Reluctantly he got up from his chair and went to the elevator, descended to the farm deck. He pushed the button on the bulkhead that would open the door and, not waiting to watch, ran straight back into the elevator cage. He dropped to the forward boat bay deck, took station so that he could keep watch on the access to No. 1 Boat. His pistol was drawn and ready.

He strained his ears to try to detect some sound other than the thin, high whine of the Mannschenn, the clatter of the innies. He was expecting to hear the shrill chitterings that he had heard before; surely *they* would be quarreling over the scraps of meat as they came down the spiral staircase. Perhaps they were all dead and he had gone to all this trouble for nothing. Perhaps. . . .

But there was somebody—no, something—coming. Something that was not thinly squealing but was making a low, moaning sound. There was the heavy padding—padding, not scuttering—of bare feet on the treads of the stairway.

It—no, *she*—came into view.

She was as he remembered her, although a little less plump. She was chewing as she moaned to herself and a trickle of blood ran from her mouth down her chin. There were half-healed scratches on her shoulders and

breasts. She stooped to pick up another meat fragment,
thrust it between her full lips.

"Susie!" cried Grimes.

She straightened, stared at him. There was no sign
of recognition on her face although, he was sure, there
was intelligence behind the brown eyes.

"Susie!"

She growled, deep in her throat, sprang for him,
clawed hands outstretched. He brought his gun up but
it was too late. She knocked it from his grasp. She
threw her arms about him in a bearlike hug and her
open mouth, with its already bloodstained teeth, went
for his throat.

It was not the first time that Grimes had been in
intimate contact with a naked woman but it was the
first time that he had been on the defensive. His head
jerked back from those snapping teeth even as her
long, ragged nails tore through the thin fabric of his
shirt and deeply scored his sides. He brought his fists
up to try to pummel her sensitive breasts but she was
holding him too closely. But he managed to get his
right hand open, found a taut nipple, squeezed.

She screamed, with rage as well as pain.

He squeezed harder, twisted.

He had room now to fight, brought his left knee up
between her thighs, felt the warm moistness that, in
other circumstances, would have been sexually stimulating—that was, he realized with a mixture of shame and
horror, sexually stimulating. Again he brought his knee
up, harder.

She broke away.

He dived for the gun but she was on him again,
the weight of her on his back, forcing his face down onto
the hard deck. With a superhuman effort he rolled over,
reversing their positions, fought his way free of her.

Again he tried for the pistol which had been kicked,
during their struggles, almost to the open door of the
boat bay. She recovered fast and hit him again, a
thunderbolt of feminine flesh that should have been soft
and desirable but that was horrifying. He was knocked

into the boat bay, fell heavily, winding himself.

He heard the thud as she fetched up against the bulkhead outside. When he scrambled to his feet the door was closing, was almost shut. He got his fingers onto the edge of the sliding panel but hastily snatched them back before they were amputated.

She must, he thought, inadvertently have pressed the local control button. Or was it so inadvertent? How much of the original Susie's own knowledge was in the brain of this replica? (Did it have a brain? He was almost sure that it did.)

He would wait, he decided, until he felt stronger, hoping that the pseudo-Susie would wander elsewhere, would not know what the pistol was for and would leave it where it had last fallen. It was not edible; she almost certainly would not touch it. And, he told himself, it would be easier to deal with this single, large opponent than with a horde of tiny horrors. (And was there a limit to its growth? Would it double in size if it ate him, Grimes? Or was its augmentation the result of a steady diet of its fellow clones?)

What was it doing now? Did it know enough? Did it remember enough to push the right button to open the door again? (But surely no cells from Susie's brain had been used in the manufacture of the original devil doll.) Were its fingers, even now, poking, intelligently or unintelligently, at the array of buttons on the bulkhead?

They were.

Grimes heard the evacuation pump start, drawing the atmosphere from the boat bay into the body of the ship. The controls for this pump were not duplicated inside the bay; the only ones that were were those for opening and closing the door. And the door, Grimes remembered, could not be opened from inside when a pressure differential existed.

He tried, of course, but it was useless.

Unless he sealed himself in the boat, and that hastily, he would not be able to breathe.

He was caught in the very trap that he had devised for the mini-Susies.

Chapter 32

Grimes activated the boat's life-support systems.

Bitterly regretting not having put on his spacesuit when he made the attempt to trap and dispose of the mini-Susies—or, as it had turned out, the life-size pseudo-Susie—he searched the boat's stores for anything, anything at all, that could be used as breathing apparatus. But he was not desperate enough to venture out into the vacuum of the boat bay with a plastic bag over his head—especially since there was little of any use that he could do once he was there.

Meanwhile, he reflected, he could survive in his prison almost indefinitely, breathing recycled air, drinking recycled water, eating processed algae that had proliferated on a diet of his own body wastes. And while he was existing drably *Bronson Star* would continue her voyage—to Bronsonia, past Bronsonia, dropping through the warped dimensions until such time as her Mannschenn Drive ceased to function. If this happened during Grimes lifetime he would be able to eject from the ship and make his way to the nearest inhabited planet—*if* he was able to fix his position, *if* the boat's mini-Mannschenn didn't break down, if, if, *if*. . . .

But he could always yell for help on the lifeboat's Carlotti transceiver and, possibly, there would be somebody within range.

And, he thought, I can yell for help *now*.

He switched on the Carlotti, watched the Mobius strip antenna begin to rotate. It would have to be a broadcast message, of course; a beamed transmission would have given him far greater range but unless he knew the exact azimuth of the target he would only be wasting time.

He said into the microphone, "Mayday, Mayday, Mayday. *Bronson Star* requires immediate assistance. Mutiny on board." And that, he thought, would tie in with the story that he intended to tell to the authorities on Bronsonia. "Master trapped in boat bay. Mayday, Mayday, Mayday."

He waited for a reply. Surely, he thought, that Dog Star liner, *Doberman*, would still be within range.

He repeated the call.

Again he waited.

He was about to call for the third time when a voice came from the speaker of the transceiver—faint, distorted but intelligible.

"FSS *Explorer* to *Bronson Star*. Your signal received. What are your coordinates, please?"

Explorer. . . . A sister ship to one of Grimes's earlier commands, *Seeker*. Survey Service. . . . A great pity that it wasn't *Doberman*, thought Grimes. Was he still on the Service's wanted list? But the old adage held true: Beggars can't be choosers.

He said, "I am holed up in my Number One boat. I am on trajectory from . . ." he caught himself just in time . . ." Dunlevin to Bronsonia. Not having access to the ship's control room I am unable to fix my position."

That last was true enough. With the boat still inboard the larger vessel it was impossible to obtain accurate bearings of any Carlotti beacons in the vicinity.

"*Explorer* to *Bronson Star*. Broadcast a steady note for precisely one minute, then returned to receive mode. Over."

Grimes made the necessary adjustments to the transceiver, broadcast his beacon call for sixty seconds, switched back to Receive.

"*Explorer* to *Bronson Star*. We are homing on you. We have you now in our MPI tank. We estimate rendezvous thirty-seven hours and nineteeen minutes from now. Can you hold out?"

"Yes," replied Grimes.

"How many mutineers are there?"

"One."

"Armed?"

"Yes," said Grimes after a moment's hesitation. It could be true. The pseudo-Susie had access to all the ship's firearms, including the pistol that Grimes had dropped.

"And you are Captain Grimes—lately Commander Grimes of this Service?"

"Yes."

There was a brief laugh. "Don't worry. We have no orders to arrest you. Confidentially, Commander Delamere didn't exactly cover himself with glory when *he* tried it on Botany Bay—and your late employer, the Baroness d'Estang, was able to pull quite a few strings on your behalf. We know that you were in charge of *Bronson Star* when she was skyjacked. What happened next?"

Grimes grunted irritably. He would just imagine those bastards in *Explorer's* control room flapping their big, ugly ears as he told his story, gloating over his misfortunes. *So,* they would be saying, *Grimes's famous luck is really running out now, isn't it?*

He said, telling the truth at first, "I was forced, at gunpoint, to navigate *Bronson Star* to Porlock. There we picked up a bunch of mercenaries and counterrevolutionaries. Then I took the ship from Porlock to Dunlevin. As you may already have heard the invasion didn't come as a surprise to the present government of Dunlevin. Two of the royalists—a ship's engineer and a catering officer—had stayed on board with me and they helped me to escape. But the three of us failed to see eye to eye about where to go next. I, of course, wanted to return the ship to her rightful owners. The other two had some crazy idea of running out to the Rim Worlds and setting up shop as a one-ship star tramp company. They pulled guns on me and ordered me to deviate from trajectory. . . ." *And that's the answer,* he thought, *to the question of why I'm ap-*

proaching Bronsonia from a slightly wrong direction.
"Cutting a long story short, there was a fight. Hodge
was killed. After the funeral I adjusted trajectory and
resumed passage. I thought that Susie—the catering
officer—wouldn't cause any more trouble. But she did."
He paused for thought. "She's quite mad, I think. Running around the ship stark naked. There was a bit of a
struggle. . . ."

He paused again, heard faintly, "Who said that
Grimes's luck was running out? *I* wouldn't complain if
I had to wrestle with naked ladies!"

"Somehow," he went on, "I was pushed into the boat
bay. She shut me in and started the exhaust pump. All
that I could do was scramble into the boat before I
asphyxiated."

A fresh voice came through the transceiver speaker,
an authorative one. "Commander Grimes, this is Commander Perkins here, captain of *Explorer*. I have one or
two questions that I'd like to ask. . . ."

Grimes had known Perkins slightly—an unimagina-
tive man, a stickler for regulations. He hoped that the
questions would not be awkward ones.

"Tell me, Commander, why you did not break
Carlotti silence until now? Surely *Bronson Star's* owners
would be entitled to learn that their ship was on her
way back to their planet."

"I feared," said Grimes, "that units of the Dunlevin
Navy might be in pursuit. I did not wish my exact
whereabouts to be known."

"The Dunlevin Navy . . ." sneered Perkins. "Two
more or less armed converted star tramps and a deep-
space tug. . . ."

"But armed," said Grimes. *"Bronson Star* is not."

"Also," went on Perkins, "the government of Dunlevin has already lodged complaint with the Federation
that you, during your escape from that world, threatened
to destroy one of their cities. Surely you realized, Commander, that that was tantamount to piracy."

"I merely pointed out," said Grimes, "that if their air

force shot me down I should fall onto a major center of population."

"Nonetheless, you disregarded orders given you by the legal authorities of Dunedin."

"I was acting," said Grimes stiffly, "in my owners' interests."

"That," Perkins told him, "will have to be argued out in the courts." His manner seemed to soften. "Strictly between ourselves, I don't think that Dunlevin's pitiful squeals will get much sympathy on Earth. Meanwhile, you can hang on, can't you, until we reach you?"

"I shan't exactly live like a king," said Grimes. "But I shall live."

Chapter 33

Grimes had time to think things over while *Explorer* sped to her rendezvous with *Bronson Star*. In some ways it was better that his rescuers should be Survey Service personnel rather than merchant spacemen. The average tramp captain, in these circumstances, would be looking out for his owner's interests—and his own. He would calculate just how much his deviation had cost, erring on the generous side, and then send in the bill. He might even claim that he was entitled to a share of the *Bronson Star* salvage money. But *Explorer's* people—even though the vessel was more of a survey ship proper than a warship—would merely be performing their normal functions as galactic policemen.

But as a galactic police Commander Perkins would be far too nosey. He would want to place the mutineer, the pseudo-Susie, under arrest aboard his own ship. In addition to the medical officer aboard that vessel there would be assorted scientists, inevitably a biologist or two. It would not take these people long to discover that Susie was not human. Awkward—very awkward—questions would be asked. And if the right answers were elicited then not only Grimes would be in the cactus but Hodge and the real Susie, probably still waiting on Joognaan for a ship off planet, would not escape the long arm of the law.

He would just have to play the cards the way that they fell, decided Grimes. Possibly, as *de facto* master of *Bronson Star,* he might be able to ride a high horse, asserting that Susie was, after all, *his* mutineer and must be placed in restraint aboard *his* ship, to be delivered by *him* to the authorities on Bronsonia. Perkins had been a little junior to Grimes when the latter had still been a Survey Service officer. Just possibly he might be able to assert his no longer existent seniority.

He slept.

There was little else to do.

He made an unsatisfactory meal from the boat's stock of preserved foodstuffs; the algae in their tanks, re-animated when he actuated the life-support systems, had not yet proliferated sufficiently to be a source of nourishment.

He had occasional conversations with Commander Perkins and his officers, discussing the boarding procedure, telling them as much as he could about the layout of the ship. He told them the code for opening the outer airlock door; he did not want them to burn their way in, causing needless damage. He was assured that *Explorer's* engineers would be able to synchronize temporal precession rates and was told that when the two vessels were almost alongside each other a transship tunnel, airlock to airlock, would be used by the boarding party.

He slept some more, ate some more, talked some more.

The time passed.

At last *Explorer* was alongside *Bronson Star*.

With temporal precession rates synchronized a switch was made to NST radio which, both in the boat and aboard the Survey Service ship, was tuned to the frequency of the boarding party's helmet transceivers. Perkins was sending his people aboard *Bronson Star* suited up, in full battle order. Any sort of scrimmage—as Grimes knew too well—aboard a spaceship is liable to result in sudden and disastrous loss of atmosphere. . . .

"Tunnel extending . . ." Grimes heard over his transceiver.

"Contact. . . . Tunnel end locked. . . . Tunnel end sealed. . . ."

Not long now . . . thought Grimes.

A fresh voice came from the speaker of the NST transceiver. *"Bronson Star's* airlock door opening. . . ." Then there was an indignant gasp. "What the hell's this? A bloody booby trap?"

I should have warned them . . . Grimes told himself.

The officer in charge of the boarders went on, obviously to Perkins, "Sir, the mutineer has tried to block off the airlock with all manner of garbage! We shall have to *dig* our way in!"

"Oh, well, thought Grimes, *that saves* me *the bother of explaining.*

"I think, sir, that we should have the gunnery officer here before we start burrowing through this mess. There could be bombs. . . ."

Grimes broke in. "There aren't any bombs aboard this ship, or even materials for making them."

Perkins said, "Commander Grimes should know, Mr. Tamworth. Get on with the boarding."

"All right for *him* to talk," came a barely audible whisper. *"He* doesn't have to stumble through shit. . . ."

There was a feminine laugh, oddly familiar. *Susie?* thought Grimes, staring around in momentary panic. But that was impossible. Susie may have laughed quite frequently but, so far as Grimes knew, the pseudo-clone was quite incapable of laughter. There was the sound again. It came from the speaker of the transceiver. *Explorer,* as a scientific research rather than a fighting vessel, would almost certainly carry female personnel on her books and those ladies must be listening in.

Some would-be humorist was singing softly,

"Down in the sewer, shoveling up manure,

That's where the spaceman does his bit!

"You can hear those shovels ring, ting-a-ling-a-ting-a-ling,

When you're down in the sewer shoveling. . . ."

"Mr. Tamworth! This is no occasion for buffoonery! Keep your men under proper control!"

"Sir." Then, still in a sulky voice, "Airlock chamber

sufficiently cleared. Access to inner door. Inner door opening. . . ."

"Proceed straight to the boat bay, Mr. Tamworth, to release Commander Grimes. Use your weapons only in self-defense."

"Sir." A long pause, then, "No sign of opposition. We are proceeding to boat bay level by elevator, which is functioning quite normally."

"You are *what?* Don't you realize that you and your people could be trapped in the cage? Get out *at once* and use the spiral stairway!"

"Sir."

"Commander Grimes, Commander Perkins here. Mr. Tamworth and his people should soon be with you."

"So I have gathered, Commander Perkins."

Finally Tamworth came back on the air. "Outside Number 1 Boat Bay. We have encountered no opposition. Am bleeding atmosphere back into the bay." A pause. "Have found one pistol on the deck outside the compartment. A Franzetti-Colt, caliber 10 millimeter. . . ." Another pause. "Pressures equalized. Am opening door."

Grimes let himself out of the boat, stepped down to the deck just as his spacesuited rescuers came in through the doorway. In the lead was a tall man with the twin gold stripes of a lieutenant on the shoulders of his spacesuit. Immediately behind him was another figure, not quite so tall, wearing commander's insignia.

This one lifted the faceplate of her helmet.

"Surprise, surprise!" she said.

"Maggie!" gasped Grimes.

Chapter 34

"Maggie!" Then, "What are you doing *here?*" he demanded.

"I'm one of the scientific officers aboard *Explorer,*" she told him.

"You might have told me that you were there," he said.

She said, "I thought it better if we didn't see each other again, John, if we didn't speak to each other, even. If Bill hadn't been so against it I'd probably not have come across to you. . . ."

"Bill?"

"Commander Perkins." Her wide mouth opened and curved, displaying very white teeth, but he sensed that she was smiling with rather than at him. "But at the last minute I insisted on accompanying the boarding party. I just couldn't resist the temptation of finding out, at first hand, what sort of mess you've got yourself into now."

"And talking of messes," said Lieutenant Tamworth, who had opened his own faceplate, "may I suggest, Commander Lazenby, that we get this one sorted out?" He handed the weapon that he had picked up from the deck to Grimes. "Your pistol, Commander?" Grimes took it. "And now, will you lead the way? This is, after all, your ship."

Lead the way? Grimes asked himself. *Where to?* Where would the pseudo-Susie be hiding? If she were hiding. . . . Where would she be lurking to pounce out on them?

The farm deck, he thought.

He climbed the spiral staircase that ran around the axial shaft, Maggie immediately after him, then the lieutenant, then four ratings, alert for the first sign of attack, pistols cocked and ready.

The farm deck was as he had left it. The boarders looked curiously at the havoc wrought by Grimes himself—the hydroponic tanks stripped of all their vegetation, the emptied yeast vats.

Tamworth said, "So this is where all that garbage in your airlock came from. . . . You said that she was mad. She must have been. . . ."

"She probably still is," said Maggie. "And, therefore, her actions will be unpredictable."

Grimes wondered why she—it—had not yet attacked, said nothing.

They continued their ascent, searching every compartment as they climbed. Storerooms, galley, pantry, the wardroom. As they looked into the Third Officer's cabin Grimes remembered his torrid sessions there with the real Susie, wondered what acid comment Maggie would make if she knew what he was thinking. But she was no more his keeper than he was hers.

They came at last to the Master's quarters.

Grimes was first into his day cabin, brought up and aimed his pistol. But the pale, naked figure sitting hunched over the desk was motionless.

"Is that her?" demanded Tamworth.

"It is," said Grimes. "If she attacks, shoot to kill."

One of the men muttered something about a wicked waste.

Grimes approached the . . . thing cautiously. It did not stir. He stretched out his left hand to touch a bare shoulder. The skin was cold, clammy. He grasped the flaccid flesh, squeezed. There was no response.

He muttered, "She's dead. . . ."

"I'm the nearest thing here to a doctor," said Maggie briskly. "Get back all of you—and you, John. Let the dog see the rabbit. . . ."

She got her gloved hands under the armpits of the seated figure, lifted and pulled until it was sprawled

back in the chair. It fell into an odd, boneless posture.
Grimes was reminded of how the homunculus that was
the start of all the trouble had looked among the shards
of its broken bottle.

"Cardiac arrest, I'd say," stated Maggie. "I can't see
any wounds. But I'd like to make a more thorough
examination. Meanwhile, Mr. Tamworth, why don't
you and your men make a check of the control room
to make sure that all is in order? And you, Commander
Grimes, stay here with me, please. I may need a little
help."

Tamworth and his men left willingly enough; in that
obscene posture the dead pseudo-Susie was not a pretty
sight.

"Shut the door, John," ordered Maggie. "Better lock
it."

While he was doing so she picked up the solidograph
of herself from the desk, looked at it. She said, "I'm
pleased that you kept this. . . . But I don't think that Bill
would be happy if he knew that you have it."

"Damn Bill!" swore Grimes.

"He's a nice bloke," said Maggie. "And he's in love
with me. Which is just as well. It means that he'll accept
my story of what's been happening here without question. You've been up to something, John, something
very odd. That thing in your chair is not human. I
imagine that you don't want it taken aboard *Explorer*
for a proper examination."

"I don't," said Grimes.

"Then talk. It's all right; I've accidentally on purpose
switched off my helmet radio. You can spill all the
beans you want without anybody but myself being
privy to your guilty secrets."

Grimes picked up his pipe from where he had left
it on the desk, filled and lit it. He noticed that the lid
of the box that he had used as a trap was open, that the
mangled remains of the first mini-Susie to be killed
were gone from it. He looked at the open, sharp-toothed
mouth of the life-sized simulacrum, shuddered.

"You haven't changed," commented Maggie. "You

can't think, you can't talk without that foul incinerator
of yours. One thing about Bill—he's a nonsmoker. . . ."

"Must you keep dragging that bastard Perkins up?"

"Why not? At least he's human. And it looks to me
as though you've been passing your lonely days and
night with some sort of obscene sex doll, something
that you picked up on some foul world whose people
cater to the tastes of woman-starved spacemen. What
happened? Did she—no, *it*—get out of control? Did
you hide in the lifeboat to escape a fate worse than
death?"

"Damn it, no!" shouted Grimes.

"Then tell."

Grimes told.

He had to keep it short. Back aboard *Explorer*
Commander Perkins must be getting anxious when
he heard no reports directly from Maggie, might even
order Tamworth and his men to break into the Master's
quarters.

Maggie interrupted once.

"Yes, John, I've heard of Joognaan, but I've never
been there. And so Susie had herself remodeled. I can't
say that I blame her if she looked like *that*. What was
she like after the job was done?"

"Not bad," said Grimes noncommitally, then went
on.

He finished, "Those surplus cells from the original
Susie must have been changed, somehow, when the
Joognaanards made me the girl in the bottle that was
Susie's parting gift. They can't have died when the
bottle was broken. They reassembled, somehow, in the
algae tank, devoured those aquatic worms. And then,
after I let them out, the horde of tiny copies of the
original thrived on the yeast. And when I tried to starve
them they reunited by absorption, or ingestion, and
grew. . . ."

"If she'd eaten you," said Maggie, "she'd have been
a giantess. But what killed her?"

Somebody was hammering on the door; either Lieutenant Tamworth was acting on his own initiative or had been ordered by his captain to ensure that Maggie Lazenby was safe.

Maggie nudged the on-off button of her helmet transceiver with her chin. "Commander Lazenby here," she said. "I'm afraid that my radio switch is defective. Unless I keep it pressed all the time it goes off. Yes, I've almost finished the examination. . . . Damn!" This latter was for the benefit of her listeners just before she switched off again.

The hammering ceased.

She said, "Poor Bill. He probably thinks that we're enjoying ourselves. But I don't think that I could with that *thing* staring at me with its dead eyes. . . . Talking of dead eyes—why did she die?"

"I can guess," said Grimes. "We know that she had a very odd metabolism. Perhaps *dead* meat was poison to her. The beef that I used as bait perhaps wasn't quite dead enough to have a lethal effect—after all, whatever comes from the tissue-culture vats is alive, after a fashion, until it's cooked. But the thing in the box—she must have eaten it—was *very* dead . . ."

She switched on the helmet transceiver again.

"Commander Lazenby here. Commander Grimes has fixed that switch for me. The woman, the mutineer, is dead. Cardiac arrest. She must have had a weak heart and the exertion and the excitement were too much for her. . . . No, Bill, I don't think that we should bring the body aboard *Explorer*. Commander Grimes has admitted that she was his mistress and still feels a sentimental regard for her. He wants to bury his own dead. . . ." She addressed Grimes. "So it's good-bye once again, John. I'm pleased that we were able to help you. We can't stay with you much longer; we have a schedule to keep. . . ." She nudged the switch again with her chin, laughed. "You never were a very good electrician, John, were you?"

She put her spacesuited arms about him, hugged him.

"Good luck, John. And good luck to your friends, to Hodge and the real Susie. You know, I'm just a little jealous of her. And good luck to you? Yes—although you still have more than your fair share of it. If *I* hadn't been aboard *Explorer,* if *I* hadn't carried out the examination of this corpse that so obviously isn't a human body, all three of you would have been in the cactus . . . ."

"Good-bye, Maggie," he said. "And good luck to you, too. . . ."

He managed to kiss her through the open faceplate of her helmet. When at last he withdrew his mouth from hers, audibly, her chin inadvertently nudged the switch.

He heard, very faintly, Perkins's voice from her helmet phones, "What was that? What was that noise?"

Maggie laughed softly, released him.

He let her out of the day cabin, said good-bye again, and good-bye and thanks to Lieutenant Tamworth. The boarding party declined his offer to see them down to the airlock. Before he went up to Control he looked at the solidograph on his desk and then at the bloated corpse sprawled in his chair. He would have to get rid of it as soon as possible; the sweet stench of decay, although faint, was already evident.

The control room NST transceiver was on. He listened to the voices of Tamworth and his men as they pushed all the garbage back into *Bronson Star's* airlock. This was not essential; as the two ships were sharing a temporal precession field transfer of mass from one to the other would have no effect. This must be, he thought, spite on the part of Commander Perkins. *Let Grimes clear up his own mess,* he must be thinking.

He looked out through the viewports at the survey ship. He could see into her control room. Maggie was not there, although Perkins was.

Perkins spoke over the NST. "You can have your ship back now, Commander."

"Thank you for your help, Commander."

"I'm rather surprised that you needed it, Grimes. You should be an expert on handling mutinies by now."

The last connection between the two ships was broken and *Explorer* faded, diminished and vanished.

Chapter 35

The first task that Grimes set himself was to rid the ship of all traces of the Joognaanard clones. After he had shut down the Mannschenn Drive he ejected the vegetable rubbish from the airlock, and then the body of the pseudo-Susie. The corpse, when he lugged it from his day cabin to the waiting elevator cage, seemed to be no more than a bag of skin filled with some soft jelly; it was indeed fortunate that it had not been taken aboard Explorer for an autopsy. Then he made a thorough search of the farm deck just in case any of the little pseudo-Susies remained, either alive or dead. He found nothing.

The distasteful but essential jobs completed he took a very long, very hot shower. He decided then to establish Carlotti contact with Bronsonia. Explorer must already have made her report to Lindisfarne Base and, even though intelligence flows very sluggishly through official channels, sooner or later the authorities on Bronsonia would learn that Bronson Star was on the way back to her home world.

He sent three Carlottigrams—one to Aerospace Control, one to Bronson Star's owners, the third to Captain Wendover, Bronsonian Secretary of the Astronauts' Guild. In all three messages he gave his ETA in Galactic Standard date and time, adding the promise, "Full report follows." The signal to Wendover also contained a query as to the well-being or otherwise of Little Sister and a request that the Guild Secretary initiate proceedings regarding the Bronson Star salvage claim.

While he was awaiting the acknowledgments Grimes

set about rewriting his report. In the original version Hodge and Susie had escaped from the ship in one of the lifeboats rather than face trial on Bronsonia. In the revised edition they had forced Grimes at gunpoint to deviate from trajectory on the passage from Dunlevin to Bronsonia. There had been a fight during which Hodge had been killed. Susie had promised to be a good girl but then, driven mad by the fear of what would happen to her when she was turned over to the Bronsonian police, had tried once again to seize the ship.

Luckily Grimes had switched on the lifeboat's log-recorder when he told his story—fictitious insofar as the latter part of it was concerned—to Commander Perkins; all that he had to do was make a transcript of his side of the conversations with *Explorer*. Luckily, too, Hodge and Susie had left almost all their personal possessions on board when they disembarked on Joognaan. Should there be a really thorough investigation all the evidence would indicate that the man and the girl had been with Grimes aboard *Bronson Star* until their respective deaths. And the boarding party from the Survey Service ship had seen a female body; only Maggie knew that it was not a truly human one—and Grimes could trust her not to talk.

The acknowledgments finally came in.

Bronson Star's owners were laconic, telling Grimes only to take up parking orbit as instructed by Aerospace Control. Aerospace Control started off by warmly congratulating Grimes on his escape and said that the full report was eagerly awaited. Wendover, too, started with congratulations.

The message went on: "Regret inform you *lerrigan* case decided in consignees' favor. Your *Bronson Star* salary garnisheed to pay court costs. Heavy damages still outstanding, also accumulated port dues and charges incurred by *Little Sister*. Have succeeded delaying forced sale of your vessel to date. Preliminary enquiries indicate no certainty of success *Bronson Star* salvage claim despite *San Demetrio* precedent. Guild lawyers awaiting your full report."

Things might be worse, thought Grimes. *Little Sister* was not yet sold—but would he, could he ever get her back? *If* he got the salvage award before the financial situation became too desperate all would be well.

If. . . .

Meanwhile, the only people who looked like coming well out of the mess were Susie and Hodge, with their changes of identity and with the money that should have gone to finance the counterrevolution on Dunlevin. If he'd had any sense, thought Grimes, he'd have insisted on taking his share of it.

It was too late now for that.

He would just have to play the cards the way that they fell.

Chapter 36

Bronson Star was once again in orbit about Bronsonia.

As before, she was hanging almost directly over that chain of islands that looked like a sea serpent swimming from east to west. But Grimes would not be aboard to admire the view for much longer. The shuttle was here with his relief and the hydroponics technician who would be making good the damage done in the farm deck allegedly by a demented Susie but actually by Grimes himself.

He handled the airlock controls from the control room, waited there for old Captain Pinner who had been the ship-keeper before Grimes got the job.

Pinner, still spacesuited but with his faceplate open and with his gauntlets tucked into his belt, pulled himself through the hatch.

"Welcome aboard, Captain," said Grimes.

"Can't say that I'm glad to be here, Captain," grumbled Pinner. "But they want you down in New Syrtis as soon as possible if not before, and I was the only one they could find at short notice to take over."

The two men shook hands.

Pinner went on, "I wish we had time for a proper talk, Captain. I'd like to hear your story about all that's been happening. . . ."

"I've left you a copy of my report," Grimes told him.

A voice came from the NST transceiver, that of the shuttle's captain. "Are you ready to transfer, Captain Grimes?"

"I'll be with you in five minutes," Grimes told him.

He went down to his quarters accompanied by Pinner. His bag was already packed but he had a quick
look around to make sure that he had missed nothing.
The old man helped him on with his spacesuit then
said, with a chuckle, "You can find your own way to the
airlock I think, Captain. I'll get back up to Control. The
best of luck to you—with the salvage claim and everything else."

"Thank you," said Grimes. "Be good."

He made his way aft, using the spiral staircase. He
paused briefly at the farm deck, watched the hydroponics technician, who had discarded his spacesuit,
working among the tanks, planting the new seedlings
that he had brought up from Bronsonia. He was un-
aware of Grimes's presence and Grimes did not disturb
him at his work.

He continued aft. He was not sure if he was glad or
sorry to be leaving this old ship. Not all his memories
of her would be bad and, if all went well, she might
prove to be his financial salvation.

Outside the airlock's inner door he sealed his faceplate, pulled on his gauntlets. He told Pinner and the
shuttle captain that he was about to let himself out,
asked Pinner to close the outer door after him. Pinner
replied rather testily that he had been a spaceman long
enough to know his airlock drill and the shuttle captain
growled, "I thought that I was going to have to come
aboard to get you, the time you've taken! A bloody long
five minutes!"

Even this airlock chamber held memories, Grimes
thought. Maggie had passed through it. (And would he
ever see her again?) He recalled the body of the
pseudo-Susie when he had placed it there prior to ejection. At the finish, the very finish, it could almost have
been that of the original woman and Grimes had felt
like a murderer disposing of the evidence of his crime.

Pressure dropped rapidly as the air was pumped into
the main body of the ship. The outer door opened. The
shuttle hung there, a mere twenty meters distant, a dark
torpedo shape in the shadow of the ship, her own open

airlock door a glowing green circle in the blackness.

Grimes positioned himself carefully, jumped.

He fell slowly through nothingness, jerked himself around so that he would make a feet-first landing. His aim was good and he did not have to use his suit-propulsion unit. As soon as he was in the chamber the outer door closed and he felt rather than heard the vibration as the shuttle's inertial drive started up.

The shuttle captain was an overly plump, surly young man.

He grumbled, "Up and down, up and down, like a bleeding yo-yo. Two trips when one shoulda done. I told them that. Lemme wait, I said, until the gardener's done his planting. Make just one round trip of it. But no. Not them. *They* want you in some sort of a bleeding hurry. . . ."

"Who are *they*?" asked Grimes mildly.

"Marston—he's manager of the Corporation. The police. Oh—just about every bastard. . . ."

"I suppose," said Grimes, "that Mr. Marston's glad to get his ship back. . . ."

The shuttle captain laughed sardonically. "Pleased? Take it from me, Captain, that pleased he is not. He'd sooner have the insurance than the ship. . . . But excuse me. I want to get this spaceborne junk heap down to New Syrtis in one piece. . . ."

Grimes tried to relax in the co-pilot's chair. (The shuttle carried no co-pilot; in fact her captain was her only crew.) He never felt happy as a passenger. His companion's handling of the controls, he thought, reminded him of that mythical monkey who, walloping the keyboard of a typewriter for an infinitude of time, would finish up writing all the plays of William Shakespeare. He transferred his attention to the viewports. New Syrtis was in view now—white spires and domes set amid green parks with the spaceport itself a few kilometers to the north. He borrowed the control cab binoculars, made out a spark of bright gold glowing in the morning sun on the dark grey of the spaceport apron.

Little Sister. . . .

"Looking for your ship, Captain? I wouldn't mind buying her myself, if I had the money. . . . But Marston's been sniffing around her. In fact he was counting on the *Bronson Star* insurance money to buy her. . . ."

The shuttle was losing altitude fast, driving down in what was practically a controlled drive. *Little Sister* and the other ships in port—an Epsilon Class tramp, decided Grimes, and something a little larger—were now visible to the naked eye.

"One thing for sure," said the shuttle captain, "Marston would sooner see you shot than getting a medal. . . ."

"Mphm."

"Mind you, he's not broke. He can afford better legal eagles than the Guild can. He'll fight your salvage claim tooth and nail. . . ."

"Mphm."

"You'da done better for everybody if you'd taken that decrepit old bitch out to the Rim or some place and changed her name. . . ."

"Not very legal," said Grimes.

"Being legal'll get you no place," said the shuttle captain. "Stand by for the bump. We're almost there. . . ."

The shuttle sat down in the corner of the spaceport reserved for small craft of her kind with a bone-shaking crash.

"Thanks for the ride," said Grimes.

"It's what I'm paid for," said the shuttle captain sourly.

Chapter 37

There was a reception committee awaiting Grimes.

Marston was there—a skinny, sour-faced beanpole of a man who looked down at Grimes with an expression of great distaste. There was the New Syrtis Port Captain who, with Captain Wendover, seemed inclined to accord Grimes a hero's welcome. There was a high-ranking police officer. There were men and women hung around with all manner of recording equipment, obviously representatives of the media.

"Captain Grimes," called one of them, a rather fat and unattractive girl, "welcome back to Bronsonia! Do you have any message for us?"

"Captain Grimes," said Wendover firmly, "will be saying nothing to anybody until he has conferred with the Guild's lawyers."

The newshen transferred her attention to Marston. "Mr. Marston, aren't you pleased to have your ship back?"

Marston tried to ignore her.

"Mr. Marston, wouldn't you rather have had the insurance money?"

Marston turned to the police officer. "Chief Constable, are you to permit me to be harried?"

"Mr. Marston," said the policeman, "these ladies and gentlemen are taxpayers, just as you are supposed to be." He turned to Grimes. "I have a copy of your report, Captain. I understand that you have urgent personal business to discuss with Captain Wendover and so I will defer my own interrogation until later. You understand, of course, that you will not be allowed to leave this planet until such time as the Police Department has completed its inquiries."

"Captain Grimes," called the fat girl, "say something to us!"

"Can I?" Grimes asked Wendover.

"Captain Grimes!" One of the other girls was aiming her recorder at him. "What happened to Prince Paul?"

Wendover had a firm hold on Grimes's arm, was obviously preparing to hustle him off. He whispered, "Tell them something—just to keep them quiet! But be careful."

"Is there any damage to the ship, Grimes?" demaned Marston.

"Only minor," replied Grimes curtly. He turned to face the reporters. He said, "I'm glad to be back. I'm gladder still to be back in one piece. I. . . ."

"That will do, Captain," said Wendover.

"I'd like a few words with Grimes," said Marston.

"*Captain* Grimes," said Wendover, "must discuss his business affairs with the Guild's legal counsel before he talks to anybody else."

"That is his right," said the Chief Constable, who obviously did not like Marston.

"I'd like to change," said Grimes. He was still wearing his spacesuit and wanted to get into the comfortable tunic and slacks that were in the bag that he was carrying.

"In my office," said Wendover.

"Do not forget," Marston said, "that the spacesuit is the property of the Interstellar Shipping Corporation of Bronsonia."

"Surely, Mr. Marston," said the fat girl, "you can afford to let the captain have a souvenir of his adventurous voyage."

The shipowner snarled wordlessly.

"Come on, Captain," said Wendover. "This way. My car."

"What was all that about?" asked Grimes during the drive to the city.

"Marston's in none too happy a financial situation," said Wendover. "Oh, he's not broke. He could still afford to buy your *Little Sister,* for example, unless the bidding were forced up to some absurd level. I happen to know that he'd like to have something like her so that he could get the hell off the planet in a hurry if—when —his financial affairs come really unstuck."

"He's not a spaceman," said Grimes.

"There are one or two drunken bums on our books," said Wendover, "whom we wouldn't recommend even for a ship-keeping job. Marston would be prepared to employ one of them as yachtmaster if he absolutely had to. And then, assuming that he did make it to some other world, that solid gold ship of yours would give him the capital to make a fresh start."

"Mphm."

The car sped through the streets of New Syrtis, came to a stop outside the dome that housed the offices of the Astronauts' Guild. The robochauffeur announced, "Gentlemen, you are here."

"We're here," said Wendover unnecessarily.

"So I see," said Grimes.

He changed out of his spacesuit in the office washroom, rejoined Wendover and the two lawyers who had been waiting for him in the Secretary's office. The four men drew coffee from the dispenser, sat around the table to talk.

One of the legal gentlemen was fat, the other was fatter. One was bald but bearded, the other practiced facial depilation but had long, silvery hair plaited in a pigtail which was adorned with a jaunty little bow of tartan silk; a not-uncommon fashion but one which Grimes had never liked.

The pigtail wearer, a Mr. McCrimmon, seemed to be the senior of the pair.

He said, "Let us not beat about the bush. Let us drive to the essentials. I understand, Captain Grimes, that you are desperately in need of money and that you hope that a successful salvage claim in respect of *Bron-*

son Star will enable you to pay your various debts and
resume possession of your own ship."

"Your understanding is correct," said Grimes.

"Then I am afried that I have bad news for you. A
claim for salvage on your behalf might, eventually, be
successful but it will be a bitter, long drawn out battle.
Captain Wendover has already suggested that we cite
the *San Demetrio* precedent but, since you did not
actually abandon ship and then return to her, this may
not be a valid analogy. . . ."

"*San Demetrio?*" asked Grimes.

"It was an interesting case," said McCrimmon, speak-
ing as though it had been heard only yesterday. "Very
interesting. The officer—who was the major beneficiary
—and his crew were, indubitably, morally entitled to
pecuniary reward and, as it turned out, also legally entitled. If they had not abandoned ship this would not
have been so.

"You are familiar with Terran history, Captain
Grimes? You will know of the Second Planetary War,
which occurred from 1939 to 1945, Old Reckoning?
Much of it was fought at sea and convoys of merchant
vessels were harried by surface, submarine and aerial
raiders. One such convoy, escorted only by an auxiliary
cruiser, a not very heavily armed converted passenger
liner, was attacked by a surface raider, a battleship. The
auxiliary cruiser put up a valiant but hopeless fight
which, however, gave the ships of the convoy a chance
to scatter as darkness was falling. One of the merchant-
men—an oil tanker, loaded with the highly volatile fuel
used by the aircraft of those days—was hit and badly
damaged, actually set on fire. Her crew abandoned ship.
Miraculously the vessel's cargo failed to explode.

"Some little time later the Second Officer, who was
in charge of one of the lifeboats, decided to reboard.
He and his men succeeded in extinguishing the flames
and eventually, despite the fact that almost all navigational equipment had been destroyed, brought *San
Demetrio* to port.

"The officer and his boat's crew were, of course,

members of *San Demetrio's* crew. They had all signed
the Articles of Agreement. Had they not abandoned
ship, had they stayed on board to fight the fires and
make the necessary repairs, they would not have been
entitled to salvage money. They would merely have been
carrying out the duties—admittedly in somewhat ab-
normal circustances—that they had signed on for. No
doubt the ship's owners would have made some kind
of *ex gratia* payment but there would have been no legal
entitlement to reward.

"It was argued, however, that as soon as they had
abandoned what was, in effect, a huge, floating bomb
the original agreement was no longer valid. Their legal
status was that of any outsiders who might have happened to board the vessel to endeavor to save her and
her cargo."

"I think," said Grimes slowly, "that I see what you're
driving at. But, as far as *Bronson Star* is concerned, was
I crew in the legal sense? I was employed by Mr.
Marston's outfit but only as a glorified caretaker. I had
signed no Articles of Agreement. My name was not on
the Register as Master."

"A good point, Captain Grimes, and one that Captain
Wendover has already raised and one that we shall
argue. You must realize, however, that it will be many
weeks before a decision is reached by the courts."

"And meanwhile," said Grimes bitterly, "I have to
eat."

"You are a rich man, Captain," said McCrimmon.
"Even only as scrap, your ship, constructed as she is
from a precious metal, is worth a not so small fortune.
My partner and I are willing to handle the sale for
you—on a commission basis, of course...."

"I don't want to sell," said Grimes.

"You may have to," Wendover told him, not without sympathy.

"You will have to," said McCrimmon bluntly. But
he, not a spaceman, would never be able to appreciate
the odd affection, the love, even, that can develop between captains and their ships.

"Think it over, Captain," went on McCrimmon. "Not that it will be necessary. The *lerrigan* consignees are already taking legal action for the recovery of the monies that you owe them."

"Well, gentlemen," said Wendover, "we have enjoyed—if that is the word—our preliminary meeting. And now, Captain Grimes, I must take you to see the Port Captain. The Chief Constable will also be present, in his official capacity. But I am sure that you have nothing to fear from them. You used force, as you were legally entitled to do, to recapture the vessel of which you were legally in change."

"And after I've seen everybody," asked Grimes, "shall I be entitled to go aboard *Little Sister?*"

"I'm afraid not. She's been sealed, as you know. She's security against your many debts. But I've booked you into the Astronaut's Arms It's not a bad pub and it's handy to the spaceport."

Chapter 38

He sat in his almost comfortable, definitely characterless hotel room. He was smoking his pipe, sipping a large pink gin, his second one. (The first he had gulped.) He looked at the solidograph of Maggie Lazenby standing on the chest of drawers. Maggie had wished him luck. He needed it.

Of course, he admitted, the situation wasn't altogether desperate. Presumably he would be allowed to sell the ship piecemeal, her fittings before the vessel herself. The autochef, for example, should fetch quite a few credits. . . .

But. . . .

He looked at the naked figurine in its transparent cube. It would be as though, he thought, he were starving and were carving hunks off Maggie to sustain his own life. A breast one day, an arm the next. . . . Then a buttock. . . . So it would be with *Little Sister*. She was a masterpiece of interior design and the subtraction of any fitting would ruin her internal symmetry.

The telephone chimed.

Grimes looked at the screen, saw the face of the hotel's receptionist. He got up, switched the instrument to reception from his end.

"Captain Grimes," said the girl, "there is a lady here to see you. May I send her up?"

A lady? he wondered. Susie's mother, perhaps. . . . What could he tell her? Dare he risk telling her that her daughter was, so far as he knew, alive, well and rich?

The almost pretty face of the receptionist was replaced by that of the unattractive fat girl who had tried to interview him at the spaceport.

"Captain Grimes—this is Wendy Wayne here. Of the *Bronson Star*." She laughed, displaying teeth that would have been better hidden. "No. Not your *Bronson Star*. The weekly paper."

"I don't feel like an interview," said Grimes.

She said, "It's not an interview I want. I've a proposition."

Grimes refrained from saying something ill-mannered.

She laughed again. "Don't worry, Captain, I've no designs on your body beautiful. I already have a lover —and *she* wouldn't approve. . . ."

"Mphm."

"Strictly business, Captain. Can I come up?"

"Yes," said Grimes.

"You've seen the *Bronson Star,* of course," she said.

"I have," admitted Grimes. (There had been a tattered copy of that scurrilous weekly aboard the other *Bronson Star,* the ship.)

"As you know, we like senational stories, preferably told in the first person. Ghosted, of course. . . ."

I Was a Sex Slave on Waldegren, remembered Grimes.

"Our readers like them too."

They would, thought Grimes.

"Your story will be sensational. There must have been some sex. That Lania, for example. . . . She had quite a reputation, you know. And that other girl, Susie. . . . With those two aboard a ship *anything* might happen!"

"It did," conceded Grimes.

"And your own name's not entirely unknown, even on this back of beyond planet. Even our media carried the news of that mutiny aboard *Discovery*. And now you're news—NEWS!—again. Unluckily we're not allowed to publish anything about the Dunlevin affair before the full inquiry's been held; too many interplanetary ramifications. That's why the wolf pack didn't really tear you apart when you landed at the spaceport today.

"But. . . ."

"There are other tales you could tell. The full story of the *Discovery* mutiny. What you did when you were captain of the Baroness d'Estang's spaceyacht. How you came to set up shop as a shipowner in that fantastic *Little Sister*. And weren't you captured by a Shaara rogue queen on one voyage?"

"So. . . ."

"So?" asked Grimes.

"As I've said, we can't publish your story of the Dunlevin adventure until we get a clearance. But we'll titillate the appetites of our readers with your earlier adventures. *On The Planet Of The Cat Women*. . . . *Space Chauffeur To the Baroness*. . . . *How My Crew Stabbed Me In The Back*. . . . *I was a Shaara Slave*. . . ."

"Mphm."

"We're willing to pay, of course."

"How much?" he asked sharply.

She told him.

He borrowed her notebook and stylus from her. He did his sums. There were the damages claimed and won by the New Syrtis Zoo, the court costs. To add to them there were the accumulated port dues and other charges. Then there was the estimated expense of putting *Little Sister* back in commission. The total came to considerably more than Wendy Wayne's offer. But there was his ship-keeping pay, which had been garnisheed. The subtraction of this did improve the situation but not enough.

He said, "I shall want more than that."

She said, "You're a greedy bastard."

"I want to keep my ship," he told her. "I don't want her sold from under me."

"My nose fair bleeds for you," she said.

He was tempted to throw this fat, insolent wench out of his room but restrained himself. After all, she represented the only chance he had to get himself off the financial rocks.

He asked, "Do you want my story—or stories—or don't you?"

"I do," she said. "My paper does. But we aren't prepared to give our right arms and a couple of legs for them. There are other stories, you know, that we can get for a damn' sight less." She took the notebook back from him, squinted at the figures that he had written down. "No," she said. "Repeat, underscore and capitalize NO."

"Your paper could put me on contract," he said. "As a sort of roving correspondent. . . ."

"Ha!" she snorted. "Ha, bloody ha! And what hold would we have on you once you lifted off this mudball?"

He said, "There's the salvage award, you know. That could be a security."

"If and when you get it. *If* being the operative word. Marston's got legal eagles who'll tear that fat slob McCrimmon to shreds. But. . . . Pour me another gin, will you?"

He did so.

"Roving correspondent . . ." she muttered thoughtfully after the first noisy gulp. "Yes. But not *you*, buster. You'll just be the chauffeur, working off the good money we've paid to get your precious ship out of hock. . . ."

"And would *you* be the *Bronson Star's* roving correspondent?" asked Grimes, his heart sinking. There are some prices too high to pay.

"Not with *you* in the same spacegoing sardine can I wouldn't!" she said. "Not for all the folding money in El Dorado. Apart from anything else, you're the wrong sex. But we've been thinking of doing an exposé on the state of affairs on New Venusberg and our Fenella Pruin is the girl to do it. And when Fenella does an exposé she often has to get out in one helluva hurry— and the schedules of passenger liners don't always fit in with her hasty departures. It cost the paper a packet to get her out of jail on Waldegren."

"The *Bronson Star* must be rich," commented Grimes.

"We're not short of a credit," she said. "Of course, most of our dirt, the really dirty dirt, is syndicated throughout the galaxy."

She finished her gin, got to her feet.

"You'll be hearing from us, Grimes. I think we can use you."

She left him with the empty gin bottle for company but he decided that he neither wanted nor needed another drink. The renewal of hope was heady wine enough. He raised his glass, in which only a few drops remained, in a toast to the solidograph of Maggie. She had wished him luck and it looked as though her wish were coming true.

But what would this Fenella Pruin be like?

He shrugged. He would cross that bridge when he came to it.

Meanwhile—and this was all that really mattered—he was keeping his ship.